DYING DAYS

ARMAND ROSAMILIA

All stories copyright 2016 by Armand Rosamilia

Cover copyright Jack Wallen

Darlene Bobich: Zombie Killer first printing February 2012

Dying Days first printing April 2011
Updated May 2016

This one goes to
The Extreme Zombie Readers...
Jeff Beesler, M.J. O'Neill and Robert
Clark
I couldn't have done this one without
you Undead Three...

And to the *real* Darlene Bobich, the
inspiration and name-sake herein...

This rerelease consists of two novellas: *Darlene Bobich: Zombie Killer* and *Dying Days*

The original covers

And now, a message from the *real* Darlene Bobich…

"I am a zombie aficionado. I have always loved the zombie genre. Something about them, the look, the idea that they just keep coming, the fact that you can shoot one and not worry about the consequences, has always intrigued me. For decades now I have imagined them. Coming in hordes or singularly down the road. Where would I go at that moment? What would I do? Would I really have what it took to shoot one? To bash one in the head with a rock? What if I looked up and saw my grandmother coming for my brains? A child? What just may terrify us about zombies is the fact that they represent humanity at its worst. Taking and never giving. Rotting and filling the world with stench and destruction. Perhaps thats what frightens us the most. They are us.

"Yet I still adore them. I appreciate the opportunity to read about Darlene Bobich the Zombie Killer. It gives me hope that when they do come down that road, I will be strong enough to slay them. Getting to know Armand and his particular brand of brainwaves has been an adventure on its own. I'm riveted, wanting it to go on and on, to never end. Keep me alive out there in Zombie World, Armand, it gives us all hope that we will have the strength to stand up to the hordes."

PART ONE

DARLENE BOBICH: ZOMBIE KILLER

Chapter One

Anything But Luck

Darlene Bobich never believed in luck. There was a reason for everything, and whether it was the good graces of God Above or skills and experience that got you through, it was never a random occurrence. Things happened for a reason, as her daddy used to say.

This morning she put a bullet through her daddy's heart. He didn't stop trying to kill her, so she put another through his stomach.

The one between his eyes and the one through his left eye stopped him.

The gun, a Desert Eagle gas-operated semi-automatic, was given to her as a gift from her daddy. This was one of the first that he'd had a hand in creating when the Israeli manufacturer had moved its operations to Maine.

A small five year window before the Desert Eagle was once again back in Israel. Her daddy had been working in a factory in Dexter making footwear for twelve years. When it was announced that better paying jobs were right in town instead of thirty miles away, he'd jumped at the chance. Her daddy knew nothing about weapons but it didn't stop him from being hired, and he was a fast learner.

Darlene remembered the look on his face when he handed her the present, a large box wrapped in Christmas paper with a silver bow. "I made this for you," he'd said and kissed her cheek. Darlene was seventeen, on the verge of graduating high school and going off to college in the fall, when he'd given it to her.

Ten years of weekends on the gun range with daddy had taught her how to handle the weapon and defend herself. She'd never needed to until the dead started to rise.

Fittingly, ironically or just plain horrifically, the first zombie she'd had to kill was her own daddy. Her aim hadn't been off; she thought that a bullet through his heart would stop him, but now she knew that his heart had given up the fight already. The second shot was meant to slow him down so she could think, but he didn't double over in pain. Pain was not an option for him anymore, only the hunger.

Darlene took the last two shots in quick succession, hitting both targets perfectly. Daddy would have been proud of the accuracy. Even as he fell, lifeless, to the kitchen floor she knew that it wasn't luck that had put this weapon in her hand and the skill to use it.

It was her sweet daddy that had.

Chapter Two

The Neighbors

There was a time for praying and a time for thinking. Right now, for Darlene Bobich, those times had passed.

She stood on her front porch, her hands shaking and the Desert Eagle brushing against her thigh in tandem. The McCrory's house across the street was on fire. Normally that would have scared her, bothered her, and maybe caused her to leap into action.

Mister McCrory, blood running down his chin, dragging his teenage daughter onto the sidewalk and ripping at her clothes while he tried to bite her, caused Darlene to hesitate.

"Has the world gone fucking mad?" she whispered. Darlene had a bad habit of whispering to herself, spilling her thoughts with no filter when she was alone. She glanced back through the open front door and sighed. Her daddy, four bullets in his lifeless body, was still in view. Absently she checked the Desert Eagle to make sure she'd loaded it again, patting her jeans pocket to make sure she had more bullets.

Darlene walked calmly across the street, ignoring all sounds from east or west. Her eyes were focused on the back of Mister McCrory's head. "Tunnel vision," she murmured. There was no way she wanted to think of what he was trying to do to his daughter. WAS GOD REALLY GOING TO LET THIS HAPPEN? TO HIS DAUGHTER, TO ALL OF THEM?

Darlene put a bullet in the back of his head, the gore splashing on the girl. His daughter was already dead. Darlene didn't even know their names, even though she'd lived across the street from these people for at least ten years.

When the daughter stirred Darlene pushed his body off of her and held out her hand, a part of her brain screaming to stop. How could she, when this child might need medical attention? She was still alive.

The teenager's mouth snapped at Darlene's fingers. Without a second's thought Darlene pulled the trigger and her forehead exploded. She fell back to the grass, now engrossed with blood.

A car alarm down the street echoed, police sirens in the distance, a scream just audible. The smoke was getting thick, billowing from the windows and opened door.

Darlene needed to run, but didn't know where. She had no real family left now. She glanced at her Toyota Tacoma pickup and smiled. "Three more payments on it."

A real laugh escaped her lips and she thought she was losing it. In the last half an hour she'd killed three people - one of them a young girl - and here she was, standing on the neighbor's lawn, with the proverbial smoking gun. Thinking about car payments.

She decided that she would stay, go back inside her house and board up the windows and doors, and get as much news as she could before the power went out or the television stations stopped broadcasting or the radio signal died.

But first, she needed to go inside the McCrory home. She was positive that the wife was home. If her husband hadn't killed her the smoke and fire might.

Or Darlene.

Rechecking her bullets in her pocket, Darlene moved across the lawn.

Chapter Three

Mall Food

The last can of tuna went down hard. Darlene wondered what had possessed her daddy to purchase twenty cans of tuna on sale. She was getting sick of tuna but with no power there weren't many choices. The stale crackers - she guessed they had been stale before the neighbors turned into flesh-eating zombies - didn't help, either.

Three weeks after she'd shot her daddy and buried him in the yard she was running out of options. They lived like any typical middle class American family: paycheck to paycheck, and grocery day hadn't come up yet before the world took a crazy turn.

She needed food, supplies, a quieter weapon than her Desert Eagle, and an idea of what was happening in the world. The power had gone out, cutting her off from the television and radio. Unlike those zombie movies that freaked her out, the streets weren't teeming with shambling, moaning corpses. She was too scared to venture out again after the debacle on the neighbor's lawn. Inside the house the undead woman had attacked her and it was all she could do to push her into the fire of her blazing home and then vomit the entire escape.

Her stomach recoiled, either from the memory or from the tuna.

Darlene decided a recon would be necessary, but where? She could list every one of her friends on one hand, and they all worked with her at the mall.

"Trip to the mall?" she whispered. She remembered when she dated Jason Nagle and he tricked her into seeing some scary zombie movie where they got trapped in a mall. Maybe that was the answer.

The drive was only forty minutes in light traffic, but she didn't know what it would be like now. It could take her five with a straight drive and no stopping, or it could be blocked off.

Or it could be gone. Darlene glanced out the window. There were plenty of smoke plumes in the air, and the fire across the street had taken down at least six houses before puttering out.

It was now or never. She had no idea what she would need besides her weapon, all the spare bullets she could carry, and her car keys. "So much for preparing for the end of the world," she muttered. She hoped the mall's power was still on so she could buy a cup of coffee and a cinnamon raisin bagel with cream cheese. "Yes, yes, that is stupid, but damn I'm hungry for something good," she whispered.

She took her daddy's F150, glad that it had a full tank of gas. She would stick to the side streets as much as possible, since the highway would most likely be crowded with cars and... She started the truck and pulled out of the driveway.

Darlene wondered if she'd ever see her house again.

* * * * *

At the corner of Main and Goddard, even though the power was out, Darlene automatically stopped for the red light. In the ten years since she'd been driving she'd never once made this light.

To her left was the Goddard Grocery, where she'd walk to as a teenager and play the Ms. Pac Man machine and buy candy. Now it was a burning husk of a building, smoke drifting and mingling with the rest of the destruction.

Darlene looked closer at the building and was shocked: two zombies were ripping apart Old Man Goddard. She couldn't look away even though she now saw exactly what they were doing.

Both zombies, obviously males, were attacking her orifices with their bloated sex organs in a grotesque parody of sex. Not content to bite her and eat her like the news had reported initially, these two seemed to be raping her. *This is insane.*

The sound was subtle at first, a dull tap on her tailgate. She glanced in her rearview mirror and her first instinct was the woman was sick from the way she shuffled.

Darlene hopped out of the truck to help but stopped when she saw the tell-tale glazed eyes and blood-ringed mouth. She got back in and put it in drive, hitting the gas pedal just as a score of undead swarmed the street to either side.

The pickup clipped one of them as she sped away and for a second she felt horrible for hitting someone. *Not some one, some thing,* she reminded herself.

* * * * *

Bangor Mall boasted Macy's, Dick's Sporting Goods, Sears and JC Penney, where she worked the makeup counter. The one-level mall had nearly eighty stores, most of which looked ransacked as she pulled into the parking lot. The far end was smoking and Macy's was just a pile of ash.

Cars stood silent in neat rows and she wondered who remained in the mall alive and who had turned into a monster. Three weeks was a long time to stay alive, although she guessed smart people would have gathered food and supplies from the mall and barricaded themselves.

Unlike the zombie movie she'd seen as a teenager, the ride over hadn't been as bad as she'd thought. The back streets were crowded with abandoned cars and she was forced to use I-95 the last few miles, but she weaved around the staled traffic and made it here.

The far parking lot seemed to be crowded with people, but they were moving slowly and she knew what that meant. She pulled up and parked in the fire lane outside JC Penneys and stared at the still-intact doors. Worth a shot.

They were locked and as a part-time associate she didn't have keys. She put her hands in front of her face and looked inside, searching for movement.

When Robin Landry appeared, just off to the right in the shoe department, Darlene ducked. She didn't want to be spotted by a zombie and especially one of her only friends. She hadn't thought of anyone else she knew turning into one of those creatures, and Robin had always been one of the only things about her job that she enjoyed.

Robin smiled and ran to the door, unlocking it as slowly and quietly as she could.

"I thought you were..." Darlene said, hugging her friend as soon as she entered and the door was locked behind them.

Robin smiled but pushed Darlene away. "I need to check you."

"Huh?"

"To see if you've been bitten."

"I haven't been." Darlene tried not to get defensive but her nerves were beyond frayed.

"That's what Nichole said, but she had a chunk missing from her leg and turned on us. We can't take chances. I'm sorry."

Darlene understood. "Frisk me."

"My pleasure," Robin said with a smile and began checking Darlene, pulling up her shirt and her pant legs.

"Lesbian," Darlene said with a laugh.

"Bull dyke," Robin said and patted Darlene on the ass. "Looks like you've been eating well the last month."

"Looks like you've been bitten on the face... oh, no, wait, that's just your ugly mug."

The two shared a laugh. Darlene looked at her friend and knew it was probably the first time Robin had laughed in weeks as well.

"Who's left?" Darlene asked.

"Only a few of us. We were all working when it started, but Ray Banner had the presence of mind to lock everything up when the newscasts started coming in. At first we fought him to let us leave but now we're glad he didn't."

"Ray Banner?"

"The cute visual manager. You definitely know who I'm talking about," Robin said and winked. "Let's get away from the doors. Most of the monsters flooded through the other side of the mall. There are dozens of them marching around near Sears."

"Do you have food?"

"Plenty. We took all of the cooking gear like the fryers and stuff and set them up in the break room."

Darlene followed Robin through the dark store. For a second it felt like another early morning shift before the store was open and flooded with customers. "What about power?"

"We're running generators in the main stockroom."

"Isn't that dangerous?" Darlene asked.

"Yes, but better than not getting a cooked meal and cold soda."

Darlene snorted. "Wow, you guys are roughing it. I've lived on tuna for three weeks, three meals a day."

"Excellent. We have tuna for you," Robin said with a laugh. They entered the office area. An older woman was sitting at the receptionist desk trying in vain to get something other than static on a portable radio.

The break room had been converted into a mish-mash of fast food cookers, soda fountains and grillers. People swarmed around the areas preparing food and serving others.

Darlene estimated there were at least twenty-five survivors, and she knew a few of them from work. The others she figured were customers.

"Grab a plate and get some food before they shut it down. After that we can go clothes shopping." Robin grinned. "You smell like shit."

Darlene got right in line, listening to her stomach growl. The smell of burgers, fries and onion rings was a nice welcome. She hesitated when the woman handing out food asked if she wanted two cheeseburgers.

"No, just one."

"Seriously? You look hungry, and this stuff will all go to rot in a couple of days. We're trying to cook it all and hand it out before it spoils." The woman glanced back. "I have about fifty burgers that need to be eaten and a ton of fries."

"Thank you. Pile it on," Darlene replied.

She finished her food and when the woman caught her eye Darlene smiled and went back up for a plate of onion rings. She washed everything down with freshly made iced tea.

"Ready to shop?" Robin asked.

"I guess." Darlene followed her back into the main area of the department store. "Why are the lights out?"

"We don't want to advertise we're here." Robin stopped. "It's not only the zombies that we're worried about, it's the looters. We lost the other part of the mall thanks to a riot and not the zombies. People are greedy bastards, you know?"

They passed a few more people, busy cleaning up and moving racks of items around.

"We're trying to board up all the doors except one and make a communal area in the middle of the store, for everyone to be comfortable. The only problem is the generators, which you can't keep wasting all the time. We only turn them on when we're cooking. Ray says if we can find more of them and get to the nearest gas station and get fuel we might be able to turn on one of the fifty-inch TV's and watch some videos, once we get settled."

"Sounds like you've got a nice plan here," Darlene had to admit. "And you've been keeping busy."

"What were you doing?" Robin asked, hesitation in her voice.

"I had to kill and bury my daddy," she said quietly.

Robin hugged her when Darlene began to cry and she was grateful for the human contact. Three weeks alone is too long.

Darlene pulled away gently and wiped her eyes. "I'm here to shop, not cry. What's on sale?"

Robin grinned. "First, let's get you a towel and a bar of soap. Go wash up and then we'll start trying stuff on. Girl, you stink."

"Sure that's not you?" Darlene asked.

* * * * *

Darlene stood in the dressing room, freshly scrubbed and wearing a matching thong and bra set, staring at her body in the full-length mirror. "A man definitely invented these giant mirrors, because no woman in their right mind wants to see every curve like this," she whispered.

Particularly troubling were the lines forming around her mouth and eyes. She was almost two years from hitting thirty but in this light she looked older. Darlene had never been a petite girl but she was far from heavy, preferring the expression 'chunky', especially her ass. She turned and looked at it in the mirror and smiled. At least three weeks of nothing but tuna had trimmed it down. The thong underwear still accentuated her shape but she'd lost some of the 'dimple' effect of her ass cheeks.

Satisfied and feeling a little better about herself, she began trying on the pile of clothes her and Robin had pulled from the racks. Try as she might to go comfort and common sense over fashion, she still managed a clingy shirt and tight jeans. After three pairs of boots she found a perfect fit, and they matched with her outfit.

Darlene began humming *You're So Vain* and giggling. She could get used to this.

"How do I look?" she said theatrically as she slid out of the dressing room area and back to the main selling floor, hands on hips and smiling.

Instead of Robin greeting her she saw a woman, blood running down the side of her face, lumbering through the children's section. At the sound of Darlene's announcement she changed course and began moving toward her.

The selling floor of the store was chaos, with zombies attacking in droves, a wave of undead coming up through the men's clothing area.

Darlene pulled her trusted Desert Eagle but didn't waste bullets, figuring if she was cornered she'd have to shoot her way out. She ran down the aisle, dodging clumsy cold hands as they reached for her, and made her way back to the doors she'd originally come in.

They were still intact but at least five zombies were in the immediate area. With no time to waste Darlene shot one of the undead in the head, the bullet passing through and shattering the glass door behind it.

Another three strides and she was outside and away from the battle waging inside. Her car keys in hand, she ran to her daddy's pickup.

At least she'd eaten and changed into a new pair of thongs.

Chapter Four

Home of the Green Monster

Even now, hiding under an abandoned car on Yawkey Way, under the shadow of Fenway Park, Darlene was in awe. Forget the five undead males ravaging a corpse across the street, ripping the limbs off and digging deeper into the body's cavity.

Darlene ignored them and stared at the green paint of the stadium, imagining the past thrills of being inside with her daddy and watching his beloved Bosox take a game from the hated Yankees. Every year they'd travel down from Maine to see at least one game and it was always against the Yankees.

As a teenager she remembered the Red Sox winning their first World Series in over eighty years and the magical hug her daddy had given her as the team celebrated on the field. Her grandfather had been a life-long suffering Red Sox fan who'd died the year before they'd won, never having seen a victory.

Something scraped against the far end of the car and Darlene stiffened. She silently cursed herself for getting emotional, and realized she'd actually been crying as she thought of the good times. *Get your shit together before you get us killed*, she thought and got her mind back into focus.

A pair of feet went by slowly, shoe-less and bloody. She watched as the zombie wandered down the street, past the bars that used to be filled with excited baseball fans. Now they were gutted and empty. Darlene would've liked to survive as long as she could in a nice Red Sox jersey and make daddy proud.

Curiosity getting the better of her, she slid out from underneath the car and made sure nothing was sneaking up on her. She ran across the street, peeking into the first open doorway. There was nothing left inside but the gutted bar and a few broken chairs.

The souvenir store next to that was free of fire damage but the looters had been thorough: not even a Red Sox sticker was left.

"Now what?" she whispered. Her run from Maine to Boston had been uneventful save the pickup running out of gas, a horde of zombies following her into Massachusetts and meager food left wherever she looked. "And no survivors."

She guessed it was familiarity and the simple looking for a safe haven that brought her to Fenway Park. Now that she was here she had no idea where to go now.

The third building was scorched but there were still bottles of alcohol behind the bar. She found a bag of pretzels - stale, but she didn't care - and a unopened can of cashews as well. Grabbing a bottle of Cruzan pineapple rum and two large Absolut vodka bottles from the shelf, she was going to have a veritable feast for dinner tonight.

Back on the street, she wondered which way to go. Back North was nothing but heartbreaking memories and her past... and cold weather coming sooner than later.

"South," she whispered. Darlene had no idea how far south she'd go or if she'd head due south. She decided to head west, into Connecticut and then into New York State until the weather told her to change course.

She looked up into the clear sky above Fenway Park and smiled. Another day and she was still alive. You couldn't ask for anything simpler, she realized. Today she had food and drink (strong drink) and just needed a place to sleep without being attacked.

"Inside the Green Monster would be a fantasy come true," she whispered. As a kid going to games she watched in amazement as the scores were manually changed for the game and out-of-town games by someone inside the tight confines of the wall itself.

One of her favorite players, Manny Ramirez, would often duck inside before an inning and she dreamed of being down there. One of her childhood dreams - besides being a ballerina, a veterinarian, and a movie star - was to work for the Red Sox changing the scores while her daddy sat in the stands with pride.

There were only a few zombies on the street and Darlene easily avoided them as she jogged around the stadium, looking for a way in. She eventually ended up at the same spot, the only possible way in to scale a fifteen foot chain-link fence with barbed wire on top.

Once again she looked up at the green stadium wall before her, perhaps in anticipation of seeing it from inside and basking in its marvel.

There was movement on top of the wall.

Darlene put her hands up to wave and get their attention, noting at least three figures, when she saw the rifles. Before she could move a bullet ricocheted off the car in front of her and slammed into the side of the stadium wall.

"I'm alive! I'm alive!" Darlene yelled as she ran back across the street and into the intact building she'd found the supplies in. Two more bullets were fired, shattering the cracked front window and taking a chip out of the doorframe.

She couldn't see the top of the wall from inside but she didn't want to chance a look and get shot. She didn't know if they were warning shots to scare her off or a bad shooter that couldn't hit a moving target. There was no way she was going to stand in the street and ask.

The first zombie came into view outside, obviously attracted to the noise. Within minutes the street was filling with them. No further gunshots rang out, which aggravated Darlene. Whoever was up there would waste bullets on the living but ignore the walking dead.

Darlene grabbed a bottle of Jack Daniels Green Label whiskey off the shelf and held it in her hand. In theory she knew she could use the alcohol for various things: as a flaming weapon, to start a fire in the event the weather turns…

"Who am I kidding? I'm going to find a hole, get drunk, and sleep it off for three days," she whispered. Darlene went in search of a back door.

Chapter Five

Fire Starter

He stood motionless, his left hand holding the small blowtorch and his right the gasoline can. He was bald, with no hair on his face or naked body. In fact, Darlene realized, he was unnaturally hairless. Even his eyebrows were gone. Despite his family jewels dangling she didn't look away. *This guy is not right in the head*, she thought.

Darlene stood in the feminine hygiene aisle of the pharmacy, about to scoop up every last tampon before her. She had just filled her shopping cart with Midol, ibuprofen, Tylenol, and ten boxes of Kleenex.

The fact that this tiny, out of the way pharmacy was not only untouched but still filled with product was too good to be true.

"I just need to stock up," she finally said.

Without a word he held up the gasoline can and shook it. She heard the gas sloshing around inside.

"Please, can I just get what I came for and go?"

He grinned, his face stretching around his pale lips. Darlene wondered how many zombies wandering around would take this crazy for one of their own.

She didn't want to kill him, and there were enough undead in the area so shooting him with her Desert Eagle wasn't a viable option.

He looked down and gently turned the gasoline can, spilling it slowly on the worn cement floor of the pharmacy.

"There's a store filled with supplies and you're going to torch it? I can't let you do that," she said and drew her weapon.

He ignored her and started splashing the products on the shelves. He still held the blowtorch, and she didn't know if shooting him was a wise decision.

"Is it in movies or real life that shit like this happens, when I shoot him and he falls and the blowtorch is still hot and the fucking building blows up and kills me?" she whispered. She didn't want to find out.

She took a step toward him when he suddenly looked up and held the blowtorch before him, still grinning. With his other hand and swung the gas can around in front of the flame.

"What the fuck is wrong with you? It's the end of the world and I have my period, dickhead."

Instead of responding he started splashing more fuel around him, coating everything in arm's length.

The fumes were starting to get to Darlene, even though this crazy bastard didn't seem fazed.

She decided to back slowly away from him with her half-filled shopping cart.

Two steps back and he was staring at her again and waving the blowtorch.

"Fuck you," she finally said and spun on her heels, trying to yank the shopping cart around as well.

The gasoline can spun overhead, aflame, and crashed against the shelf she'd previously been shopping at. The fire crawled up and down shelf like a hungry spider, catching cardboard boxes.

Darlene had no choice but to abandon the supplies and begin running, wondering if he would give chase.

At the front counter, just before reaching the door, she stopped and turned, hoping if he was behind her she'd surprise him.

Instead, she heard him tossing entire shelves to the ground.

"Sick fucker," she whispered.

The flames were already engulfing the section and smoke billowed to the roof, found nowhere to go, and began spreading.

Darlene grabbed a small hand basket from next to the counter and filled it with as many candy bars, small bags of chips and warm sodas as she could fit.

"Bingo," she cried when she saw the travel packs of tampons and medicine behind the counter.

She lunged across the counter and made room in her basket by discarding melting candy bars, and filled it, stuffing her pockets with Advil singles.

Before she could leave he was suddenly in the nearest aisle holding a flaming tube of gift wrap. The grin hadn't left his face as he waved it around.

"Fuck you," Darlene finally said and pulled the Desert Eagle. At this point she'd rather face a horde of undead than this psycho. "Dickhead."

She put a bullet just above his eyes, right where his eyebrows used to be. He hit the ground, the wrapping paper falling and igniting the gasoline on his feet and legs.

Even dead he was still grinning.

Chapter Six

Ladies Night In Buffalo

The Rusty Bar proclaimed, via the blood-streaked sign on the intact door, the best buffalo wings in the world. Darlene doubted she'd get a chance to try them. At this point a handful of ketchup packets would be heaven.

Moving across the northeast in a normal world was hard enough, but adding zombies, looters and blocked main roads and you had a heck of a time getting anywhere.

"And now I'm in fucking Buffalo and I'm cold," she whispered. She was grateful it wasn't winter and there wasn't three feet of snow on the ground. She knew the snow could pile up out here just like in Maine. She was only wearing jeans and a T-shirt she'd gotten weeks back after the attack at the mall. Already her boots were scuffed and the soles beginning to wear down.

Finally, feeling stupid for standing out here in the cold and exposed to undead, she tried the door and smiled when it opened.

Before she'd gotten two steps inside she felt the cold steel pressed against the side of her head. "Freeze."

"Not a problem," Darlene said, making sure whoever had the gun to her head could hear her. Zombies didn't talk.

"Hurry up inside but keep your hands up where I can see them."

"It's dark, I can't see," she said.

She was pulled roughly inside and she heard the door shut and barred. A light was suddenly thrust into her eyes as two different sets of hands rummaged through her meager supplies, stripping her backpack from her shoulder. She felt her Desert Eagle, cold against her back, as it was pulled out and taken. The entire time the gun was still to her head.

"Talk," the voice said.

"I'm just hungry and passing through. I'm trying to survive just like you, alright?" Darlene closed her eyes, bright white spots blinking from the flashlight. At least they were talking. She figured as long as she was holding their attention they wouldn't pull the trigger. "Obviously I came to the wrong bar."

Someone snickered and the light was shined down to the worn floor.

"Follow me." The light began to move so Darlene followed, knowing there were at least two people behind her and one ahead.

A door was opened and candle light spilled from it. She realized she had originally been in a small hallway and was now in the main bar area, where at least thirty heads looked up at her.

"Have a seat right there," the man who was leading them said and pointed to a single chair against the wall. "Doug will be back shortly."

No one spoke as she sat. She noticed only three women present and they looked beaten-down and scared. One of them, an older blonde, was staring at her with a strange look on her face. Darlene smiled at her but she looked away.

"I'm Rusty, and this is my bar." He was in his late forties, a rough and tumble-looking Good Ol' Boy, with an American flag tattoo on his shoulder. He wore a faded denim sleeveless jacket and matching blue jeans, his Buffalo Bills hat on backwards. His beard was scruffy but Darlene figured his look had nothing to do with the end of the world. Zombies or not, this was a guy who was right at home with the chaos.

"Pleased to meet you, Rusty. Nice place you have here," Darlene said and offered her hand. He looked at her with a smirk and ignored the gesture. Someone sitting at the bar said something and everyone laughed, watching the awkward exchange.

"Hungry?" Rusty asked her.

"Yes, but not if it's a bother. I'm actually just moving along, decided to check out the place before I headed out," she said. Darlene was getting a bad, bad vibe from these people.

Rusty stared at her for a minute, slowly looking her body over. "No trouble at all." He turned away and walked past the loud group at the bar, sure he heard Rusty say 'dibs' as he disappeared into the back room.

I need to leave. *No way I'm going to be this guy's bitch,* she thought. She was about to make a run for it when she realized her Desert Eagle and backpack were gone. She wouldn't get far without them.

The guy who'd led her in was nowhere to be found and scanning the room only elicited catcalls and rude comments, loud enough for her to hear but never directly at her.

Rusty returned with a paper plate overflowing with food: French fries, Buffalo wings, coleslaw and baked beans. "Southern cooking, just like mama used to make," he said with a laugh. "Sorry, but we ran out of silverware."

"Thank you," Darlene said. "It looks delicious."

He smiled with genuine pride. "Made it all myself. The fancy place up the road might be credited with making the first Buffalo wings but I make them best."

She waited until he walked away to begin digging in with her fingers, savoring the rich taste of each item. He was a damn fine cook and she had the briefest thought of staying here and trying to fit in. When she looked up from her half-finished plate her last swallow was caught in her throat.

The bar had gone silent and everyone was openly staring at her, waiting for something. The woman looked at her with that expression again and Darlene realized it was with relief. The woman was actually smiling when Darlene began to feel woozy.

* * * * *

Darlene woke, in the fetal position, on a dirty mattress. Her clothes were gone and her body felt like one big bruise. Her mind felt fuzzy around the edges, like she'd taken too much cough syrup.

She rolled over onto her back and felt nauseous. A quick, painful spin to her side and she was throwing up onto the floor.

"You'll have to clean that up yourself."

Darlene saw the woman, the grinning bitch, from the bar. She was sitting patiently in a chair near the closed door, with Darlene's clothes in a neat pile on her lap. Next to the leg of her chair was a wash basin, soap and a small bottle of shampoo.

"What happened to me?" Darlene asked, wiping the vomit from her lips.

"What do you think? You're the new favorite. Wash up, get dressed, and meet me in the kitchen in ten minutes. You need to cook." The woman rose and went to the door but turned back, a look of disdain on her face. "Enough with your lazy fat ass lying around here."

* * * * *

Rusty stepped between Darlene and Ginger, keeping the women at arm's length. "Enough, or you know what happens."

Apparently Ginger knew it would be bad and not an idle threat because she immediately put the saucepan down and went back to washing the carrots.

Rusty pulled Darlene to the back of the kitchen. She winced when his grip found one of her many bruises. "I need you to settle down."

"You have to be kidding. These bitches are mad at *me*! How fucked up is that?" Darlene said.

Since yesterday she'd had it equally as rough. After getting cleaned up and dressed and crying until no tears would come, she went to the kitchen in hopes of finding a knife. Her goal was to rally the other women - even the bitch - and bust their way out from these madmen. Instead, she'd been attacked by the women, clearly jealous of her and how the men were now favoring her. When the dust had settled she was beaten by two psycho rednecks and locked in the walk-in freezer (which didn't have power, luckily) for hours until she 'learned to play nice with the other whores'.

Darlene decided to bide her time, learn as much as she could about the group, and try to find a weakness. She also wanted to find the bastard that took her Desert Eagle.

She spent the day cleaning vegetables and cutting potatoes for the communal soup they were making. Including Ginger (who kept her distance but shot dirty looks at her whenever she could) and the bitch (who she overheard being called Barbara), there were five other women in the bar but they ignored Darlene and went about their business.

Rusty came in right before the soup was done and watched Darlene work. The other women became clearly agitated by the intrusion but said nothing.

Finally, as Darlene handed over her part of the food and cleaned up her countertop, Rusty approached her. "Doug wants to see you."

* * * * *

Doug Conrad was not what Darlene had expected. With the group of men in the bar area, she'd seen a common thread: rednecks from the frozen wastes of northern New York State or down from Canada, farmers and hunters and inbred pieces of shit that thought with their dicks and/or their rifles.

This guy was a foot above them, both physically and mentally. He wore an American flag sweatshirt, his baseball cap with *SoTNP* stitched on it and striped in red, white and blue. He carried himself with a swagger, a self-confidence, she hadn't seen in a man in a long time. He wasn't a hillbilly or a redneck or a Good Ol' Boy, he was… powerful.

"I understand you had a problem with Ginger?" he asked, a thick New England accent.

"Ginger had a problem with me," Darlene said.

Doug looked past Darlene and addressed Rusty. "Let Ginger know we won't be having anymore problems. Understand?"

"Yes sir," Rusty replied and left.

Doug sat down on a chair at a small table. They were in the bar offices. He motioned for her to join him.

She sat across from him and tried to relax. "I thought this was Rusty's place?"

"It is." Doug smiled and despite the situation she smiled back. He didn't have the look of a predator like the rest of the men here. He didn't look desperate or wild. He looked refined, educated, and manly. "But I'm running the show."

Darlene was smitten with him and she felt her face grow hot. His intense eyes locked on hers and she looked down at her hands.

"Tell me about yourself. You're not from Buffalo."

"No, I'm from a little town in Maine called Dexter. It's close to Bangor."

"What are you doing so far west?" he asked.

"Trying to survive." Darlene grew angry and looked up, meeting his gaze. "Why am I being held here?"

Doug locked his fingers and leaned forward, putting his elbows on the table. "No one is a prisoner, but it's not safe out there. The city is overrun, and it's amazing you got this far."

"I want to leave."

"When I feel it's safe."

Darlene leaned forward and tried to look tough, even though she was shaking inside. "So I'm your prisoner."

Doug stood and scowled at Darlene. "I'm the only thing keeping you alive right now. I would remember that."

"What happens if we're attacked? How will I defend myself?"

"Defend? You're a woman. The men will protect you, and in exchange we offer you food and shelter and life. I'm not sure why you aren't thanking me right now," Doug said.

"Seriously?" Darlene wanted to scream. "I just want to leave."

Doug turned away from her. "Jesse, come get her back to the kitchen, please."

"What if I refuse to be your cooking bitch?" Darlene demanded as she stood. "What if I try to leave?"

Doug moved so quickly she didn't have time to react. His fingers were wrapped around her hair and she was dragged to the ground with such violence that she nearly blacked out.

He got close to her face, keeping his grip. "You will do what you are told or you'll end up like all the rest of the bitches that decided that the Sons of The New Patriots weren't worth living and dying for. Understand?"

Doug dragged her up by her hair just as Jesse came in with a grin.

Darlene, dazed, was pulled by Jesse out of the room. She did, however, notice that Jesse was the prick that had taken her Desert Eagle and had it tucked into his waistband.

She decided that she'd kill him first and then Doug.

* * * * *

During the course of the last twelve hours Darlene played 'nice' with the other women - completely ignoring them unless she absolutely needed a pot or utensil - and prepared one meal after another. From listening to the idle chatter in the kitchen she figured out that there were actually eighteen women in the bar and adjoining houses, sixty-five men (all members of the Connecticut-based militia group Sons of The New Patriots) and another ten men who foraged for food and supplies.

From the growing pile in the walk-in it was obvious they were doing a great job. An hour ago one of the men wheeled in a shopping cart overflowing with canned goods, and the women began picking through it.

Barbara was head of the kitchen and she barked orders, setting the menus and giving tasks to the women. If she weren't such a bitch Darlene would've asked her if she'd been a cook or restaurant manager before all this. She clearly knew what she was doing.

Ginger was absent and no one said a word, but they all equally ignored Darlene.

A slight banging to her right startled her. When she looked over all she saw were storage boxes piled to the ceiling. The noise came again.

"What's the problem?" Barbara said and approached.

"Something's knocking."

Barbara turned and yelled. "Jesse, we got us another one in the alley."

"Got it."

Barbara looked at Darlene. "Get back to work."

Five minutes later Darlene heard a muffled gunshot from outside and glanced at the pile of boxes. She wondered if she could get through the pile and through whatever door was there before she was chased.

When Jesse came back he smiled at her and waved the Desert Eagle. "This baby can shoot. One shot and his freakin' head blew off." Jesse put the weapon back in his waistband. "Plus, Ritter found me so much ammo for this baby I could probably shoot my way out of Buffalo."

It took everything for Darlene not to charge him, knowing he was trying to get a rise out of her. Instead, she went back to work peeling potatoes.

Jesse came up to her and waved the weapon at her. "So close and yet so far away, right?"

Barbara came up slowly on Jesse with a look of distress on her face. "Jesse, please leave the kitchen."

Jesse ignored her, staring at Darlene, eyes wandering over her body as he licked his lips. "I wonder what you'd do to get it back?"

Barbara put a hand tentatively on his shoulder. "Please, you need to go."

Jesse grabbed Barbara in a headlock and put the gun to her head before she could react. She began screaming. He smiled at Darlene again. "I bet if I shot this bitch in the head you wouldn't even blink, would you?"

"Please don't," Darlene said quietly. As much as she hated the women she had no desire to see her head blown to pieces, and especially if she unwittingly had something to do with it. "Just let her go and you and I can talk."

"Talk? Fuck that noise, bitch. We'll be bumping and grinding before the night is through."

Jesse released Barbara and knocked her on the floor. "Stay there, bitch, or I will shoot you. I don't care what this whore says."

"But you'll care what Doug says," Rusty said from the doorway, a .357 in hand. "Secure that weapon and get over here."

Jesse leaned forward at Darlene as he raised the Desert Eagle. "We'll continue this later, and that fat ass of yours will be mine."

"Now, Jesse. You were told she was off-limits." Rusty held out his left hand, the right still holding the gun at Jesse. "Hand it over."

"Bullshit."

"Fine." Rusty smiled. "I'll let Doug know you were messing with his property and refused a direct order from his second-in-command. Where do you think that will get you?"

"In the pit," Jesse said quietly.

Rusty went nose-to-nose with Jesse. "I didn't hear you, soldier."

"Sir, in the pit, sir," Jesse said. He handed over the Desert Eagle. With one final nasty look at Darlene he left the kitchen.

Rusty stared at the women for a full minute, no one speaking. Finally he motioned for Barbara to get up. "Back to work, you all just got us behind. No food for you tonight if you don't hurry the fuck up."

* * * * *

Darlene didn't move a muscle, pretending to sleep. She figured Barbara and Jesse would both go after her much sooner than later and she'd be ready. Barbara had the easiest means since she was cramped in the same room as Darlene and another six girls. Darlene was rolled up with a thin bed sheet in one corner, facing the dark figures and listening to them snore, shuffle and moan in their sleep.

Her anger and frustration kept her awake and kept her going. She knew to relax would get her killed, and crying or accepting the hopelessness of her situation would destroy her, so she embraced the raw power and tried to use it.

As silly as she knew it was, she remembered the time when she'd first gotten the job in the makeup department in the mall. Her community college had stalled and she still hadn't figured out what she wanted to do in life. After a long talk with her daddy she decided to take a break for a semester - as much as he was against it - and get a real job. Her daddy paid all the bills, but she knew it was way passed her time to add something positive to the household.

She remembered kissing him on his cheek as he sat there wringing his hands and staring at the microwave. She told him about being in her mid-twenties and never having worked a real job save the fast food ones when she was a teen, her job at the library in college and her brief two-week work as a hostess in that seedy restaurant outside of Dexter.

Her first real job brought her the harsh realities of life: not everyone liked you or was straight up real with you or just had so much jealousy that they were hard to be around.

Winnie was the assistant manager of the department, a ten-year veteran who'd been stuck behind the department head for four years. She had a bad attitude for the new people coming in and no patience to train, yet every complaint up the chain fell on deaf ears.

After four months of Winnie undermining associates, doing underhanded things with their commission sales and changing schedules at a whim, Darlene had had enough.

She didn't care if she lost her job at that moment because she was so stressed. She met Winnie in the parking lot after a closing night shift and without preamble, crowded the woman against her car. "What the fuck is your problem with me?" Darlene said, amazing herself at her rage. Her original point was going to be to try and talk to the woman one more time before quitting, but as the anger built all shift and Winnie acted like a typical bitch, she couldn't control it.

Darlene didn't remember the rest of the confrontation that night, but she did smile at the outcome: Winnie went out of her way to be nice to her, giving her prime shifts, siding with her when the new girl Julie was trying to steal sales, and chit-chatting with her whenever possible.

Movement in the darkness brought her back to the present and she tensed up her body. A shadow pulled itself from the far corner, where Barbara had set up to sleep.

Showtime, she thought and slowly pulled the butter knife from under her pillow. When the figure got within three feet of her Darlene suddenly sprang, driving a shoulder into her opponent's midsection and wrapping them up as they plunged to the floor.

Darlene had gone over this a dozen times in her head and she was ready: she drove the butter knife into her throat, knowing if she hesitated or showed mercy she'd be dead.

Chaos erupted around them as flashlights and candles lit the scene while the women in the room moved to escape the battle but get into a good position to see it.

By then it was over. Darlene, on all fours, had the knife plunged into the neck of an unmoving woman. Not Barbara.

Confused and shaking, Darlene looked around and finally caught the smile of Barbara, standing at the door. Before Darlene could do anything Barbara left.

"Who is that?" Darlene finally asked as she stood, her legs threatening to give out. Her stomach roiled and she puked against the wall. Her chest and arms were covered in blood and she could only stare, spittle dripping from her lips, as the woman went into convulsions on the floor.

Darlene was going down, her vision dimming, but as she began toppling she felt rough, strong hands grabbing her and dragging her past the scene of carnage. Her feet slid through the pool of blood as some women screamed and others sobbed.

In the hallway she closed her eyes and puked again as someone lifted and fireman carried her. She was dumped onto a mattress. When she opened her eyes Rusty and Doug were standing over her. She threw up again, too weak to even roll, just coughing it out of her mouth so she didn't choke.

Rusty, a look of torment in his eyes, came to her and gently lifted her head. She watched as Doug folded his arms behind them and smiled wickedly.

Lucky for her Rusty's first punch to the jaw knocked her out.

* * * * *

Cold. Darlene felt her body shuddering and wet. Her thoughts were jumbled, fuzzy around the edges. When she opened her eyes she wasn't surprised to see the entire bar staring at her, led by Doug, Rusty and Barbara. She was outside, it was nighttime, and she could hear the undead clanging against chain-link fences nearby.

They let her stand. "Seriously? Naked again?" She threw up her hands in disgust and ignored the laughing and catcalls. Turning to Doug she looked at him with what she hoped was utter defiance. "Do your worst, dickhead. Just remember one thing: I'll have the last laugh when I'm shooting you in the fucking head."

Doug grinned. "I seriously doubt that, sweet ass. In fact, after everyone else here has gotten their turn in with your body, it will be my turn. The last turn."

"I'm first, since I owe that bitch," Jesse said and strode forward. When she tried to run away hands grabbed her from behind and forced her to the ground on her back.

She stopped struggling and put her legs up. "Hurry up, Minute Man. There's a line behind you," she said loudly.

As everyone began to laugh she could see that she'd gotten to Jesse, which is what she wanted. She knew this was the end of the road for her, and she'd be raped and killed but she didn't want to go out crying and feeling powerless. Even though her stomach threatened to spill and she was shuddering, she tried to push it down defiantly.

When he pulled his jeans down she laughed. "Did you forget your dick inside the bar? I'll wait here while you go fetch it."

Jesse was on her suddenly, his pants down. He was fumbling to get inside her, glaring at her with venom. "I'm going to rip you open, you fucking bitch," he said quietly.

"Doubtful," she said but turned her head. She noticed the undead trying to get through the chain-link fence, the padlock keeping them out.

Jesse was still struggling as she turned the other way, seeing the same thing the other way down the road: undead behind the fence.

"You done already?" Darlene said and smiled at him when everyone began to laugh and cat-call.

Jesse raised up on his elbows, then to his knees, bringing his hand up to slap her. Instead, Darlene kicked up with her knee and connected with his groin. As he fell to the side she reached up, using him as a shield, and reached around his back.

She pulled her Desert Eagle just as she heard the scrambling around her. Instead of attempting to use Jesse as a hostage - she knew they could care less about him - she pointed and fired at the lock on the gate, using every ounce of training her daddy had ever given her with her weapon.

Before the lock was even on the ground she'd turned and shot the other side.

Jesse bucked on top of her as someone put two bullets in his back.

Darlene began firing at anything around her, sure she'd be shot at any moment. Instead, they scattered around her as the zombies breached the gates.

A man tripped over Jesse and Jess slid off of her. She crouched, still firing, until her gun was empty. A quick search of his jeans pockets and she found loose bullets and a full box.

She stood and looked for Doug, Rusty and Barbara, hoping to see them so she could kill every last one of them. Instead, it was such chaos that she couldn't tell living from dead.

Swearing to someday find them, she pushed her way through the crowd, loading and firing as she moved, and clearing a path.

Darlene's anger got her safely down the street. She was naked and bruised but she was alive. And she had her Desert Eagle back.

Chapter Seven

Clothes Shopping

Darlene Bobich didn't know which part was worse right now: being naked on the cold streets of Buffalo, New York or the fact there was a zombie apocalypse happening all around her.

She decided that in the 'right here, right now' the freezing naked thing took precedence over the undead thing, so she tried doors and windows as she made her way down a suburban neighborhood that had been relatively unscathed. Here and there a home had been torched and most of the cars on the street were demolished, but the lawns were overgrown but not trampled like she'd seen everywhere else.

Houses, dark, stared back at her. To her right a pickup truck, doors open, was halfway backed out of the driveway. Across the street the front door had been ripped off its hinges and propped against the bushes.

Darlene realized the block reminded her of home, even though she was hundreds of miles away. The pretty, well-kept middle-class block, rows of likable houses. She imagined the kids coming inside just before dark, mom fixing dinner while dad pulled up in his Camry and parked next to mom's mini-van.

Her daydreaming was shattered by the crash of glass somewhere close by. She ran across the street and up the driveway since the house looked still intact.

The front door was locked and she heard footsteps, slow and methodical, from the street. Without streetlights and with only the thin moon above everything was in silhouette, but she didn't need to see to know there were undead in the area.

Darlene ran to the garage side of the house and around through the side yard, careful not to crash into the low bushes or make any noise. The side door was locked as well, but not the back gate to the yard.

She entered, Desert Eagle drawn, hand shaking, with only moonlight for a guide. Every shadow moved and attacked her and she had to stop and close her eyes and breathe before she panicked.

"Nothing but the ghosts," she whispered. "And my nerves." Darlene made sure the gate clicked back in place.

The back patio was strewn with leaves but otherwise untouched, the table and chairs waiting for the nearby grill to get started so the family could eat. The sliding glass doors were locked, the shades inside drawn.

Darlene was standing there, gun in hand, nothing on, trying to come up with a game plan but her mind was blank. She didn't think she could stay in the yard all night like this. It wasn't freezing out but it was getting colder the later it got.

The low growl near her ankles scared her so much that she slipped on the patio and fell to the ground, her weapon hitting the grass.

When the large dog stood over her she thought she would either be bitten or it would bark and she'd be attacked by a horde of zombies. Instead, it sniffed quietly at her hand. She let the dog smell her and was relieved when its tail began to wag.

"Where'd you come from, boy?" she asked, petting the German Shepherd. The yard was completely fenced in. Darlene went back to the sliding doors and looked around for a pet door or something she'd missed. Nothing, but it was so dark.

"Throw me a bone, boy," Darlene said and then giggled at her stupid pun. The dog sat on its hind legs and stared at her, tail going a mile a minute.

She felt around and found an opening to the far left of the door, next to the start of the bushes. It was larger than a normal doggy door but she didn't think she'd be able to squeeze through. "Not with these hips," she whispered.

"Go inside, by, and unlock the door for mommy," she whispered at her new friend, but he only licked her hand. "Didn't think so."

Darlene didn't hear any noise from over the fence, only the sound of the dog breathing. It sat down on its hind legs and stared at Darlene, tongue wagging.

"After you?" Darlene said to the dog and pointed at the small opening. When he didn't jump in front of her -*typical male*, she thought - she got down on her hands and knees.

"Let's get this big ass through the tiny hole," she whispered. "That's all I'm asking."

She wished again she had a flashlight, because when she pulled the flap open and squeezed her head in it was pitch black. Her shoulders squeezed in and she managed to get her chest through with difficulty, but once she got to her hips - damn Bobich Family curse! - she was screwed.

Of course, that was the moment the dog began to growl low and mean.

Darlene, panicking, tried to push herself back out but she was firmly stuck. *I'm going to die, trapped in a doggy door, all alone*, she thought. *Of all the shitty ways to die.*

Something brushed against her leg and she stiffened. She hoped it was only the dog. A strange, calming thought came to her just then: she wondered what the dog's name was. Maybe he had a tag on his collar.

Darlene closed her eyes, since she couldn't see anyway. Very slowly she started to rock her hips, her hands pushing against the sides of the wall as she did.

"Please don't bark," she whispered when she heard him growl again, right behind her on the steps. There was another noise, but it was so muffled and she was inside the house that she wasn't sure she'd actually heard it or not.

She tried turning her hips on an angle and pushing her way in. She was sweating. *Look on the bright side: at least I don't have clothes on to hinder me more.* She wiped her thick mop of soaking hair with her hand and went to touch the floor when she stopped.

It was quite humid in the house. There was no telling how long the power had been out and the family closed up the house. It was hot. Darlene started wiping her face, neck and hair and rubbing whatever parts of her hips she could touch.

She rocked back and forth again, and after what felt like six hours but was likely six minutes she was free. Pulling her legs in, she turned and held the door open.

The German Shepherd was growling at something she couldn't see, stepping forward with head raised and teeth bared.

"Come on, boy, come inside," she whispered. "Come to me."

The dog barked, once, loudly.

"Shit." She knew she'd be pushing it if she tried to get back outside to grab the dog. She put her head back out and looked around, but she didn't see anything or anyone. Of course it was still so dark outside that she couldn't see past the back patio.

"Please, please, please, come here," she whispered.

The German Shepherd stopped and looked at her. She smiled and waved her hand at him.

She heard the gate being pushed slowly open.

The dog started barking and moved out of her sight.

Darlene came fully inside the house and stood, holding onto the Desert Eagle. She looked at the sliding glass back door, currently covered in shades, and nearly punched herself in the head. "Stupid bitch," she whispered. *The fucking door is right here. I'm still crawling on my hands and knees from* inside *the fucking house.*

She clicked the lock to the door at the same time she moved the shades using the Desert Eagle. The dog was lost in shadows but she could hear him growling and barking.

The door slid on its hinges with a slight squeak. She froze, the door only half a foot wide. Cool air entered the house and brushed against her naked body, cooling her off. The sweat still on her hips and sides gave her goose bumps when mixed with the night air.

Darlene could clearly hear footsteps now on the lawn, moving toward the patio. She moved back into the house, angling so she could still see out the crack in the door and fire if need be.

"Calm down, little doggie," she heard a gruff male voice say. "You'll alert the damn neighborhood."

"Just shoot the damn thing," a whispering female voice said with disdain.

Is that Barbara and Doug? She started to sweat.

She watched the figure kneel and pet the dog, who stopped growling and barking. "Traitor," she whispered but knew the dog was starved for attention. Another figure, obviously the woman, was suddenly next to him.

"Let's try the house," she said. "I don't like it here."

Darlene took several steps back before turning. Her eyes had gotten adjusted to the gloom and she could just make out darker objects - the living room couch, the entertainment center, and the coffee table - and avoided them as she scampered down a hallway and looked for a place to hide.

She heard the sliding door opening as she entered the bathroom, closing the door behind her as quietly as she could. *Stupid move,* she thought. *Trapped myself in the bathroom. Naked.*

Darlene climbed into the bathtub and pulled the shower curtain closed, pointing the gun in front of her. Hands shaking and trying not to cry, she slid down into the cold tub and waited.

The couple - she was sure it wasn't Barbara and Doug - began moving about the house but so far neither had bothered entering the bathroom. If they did she would simply shoot them.

There were no windows in the room and the darkness enveloped her. As a little girl she'd never been really scared of the dark, only when it suited her needs and she wanted to get closer to her daddy. They'd vacationed in Vermont a few weeks after her mom had died, daddy so quiet and sad. They spent a week in the woods, in a small camper, getting back to nature. Fishing and canoeing. Daddy had cried softly that first night, wrapped in his sleeping bag with the camper top open to the stars. Darlene had feigned being scared of bears and climbed in next to him. He stroked her hair and sobbed quietly until she was fast asleep.

* * * * *

Darlene woke with a stiff neck. She had to pee and laughed at the stupidity of that. *I'm in a fucking bathroom.* She stretched, rubbing her muscles. Her legs and arms were needles and pins. There was no way to tell what time it was, but from the way her body felt she'd slept for a few hours at least.

Not that it helped. She felt more exhausted than when she'd broken into the house. *Crawled into the house.*

After taking care of personal business (and enjoying the comfort of an actual toilet and toilet paper) Darlene crept to the door and put her ear to it. She didn't hear anything, idly wondering if doing this actually worked outside of movies.

At this point, lured into a false sense of security, our heroine opens the door and the chainsaw-wielding maniac in the dead skin mask attacks, she thought. "Better than crouching naked in a bathroom until you starved to death," she whispered and opened the door a crack.

The hallway, of course, was dark, but there was a faint natural light tint to everything. She guessed the sun was up. She opened the door and stepped out into the hall but she wasn't attacked and she didn't hear a sound.

Back into the living room she wasn't surprised to see the sliding glass doors closed and locked. The couple was still in the house.

Her initial urge was to simply leave and find another house to search, but she needed clothes now. She knew it was stupid and made no real sense, but she walked back down the hall and opened a door at the end of the hall.

The couple was there, completely naked, lying on top of the bed covers. They were both filthy, with small cuts and bruises covering their arms, face and legs.

Darlene, holding the Desert Eagle, went to the closet, which was slightly ajar. She fingered through the hanging clothes, finally settling on a green blouse, at least two sizes too big. *Great, I find the house that the Chubby Family lived in.* None of the clothes would fit her comfortably, and the pants were way too big, even if she had a belt on.

She turned when she heard one of them moving on the bed and was not surprised to see the man, .357 in hand, sitting up.

They stared at one another but when his eyes lingered to her naked body she turned and gave him a full view and smiled. "I just wanted clothes," she whispered.

"This is our house," he said loudly. The woman stirred and woke, frowning when she saw Darlene.

"It's not your house. I got here about ten minutes before you did last night."

"Bullshit. We been here for hours," the woman said. "Put some damn clothes on before you give my husband a heart attack."

Darlene didn't point out the obvious: that the woman was also naked. Instead, she stared at the man. "I'm not here for trouble; I just wanted to find clothes."

"Yeah, well, fat people live here… lived here. We're just passing through as well." He smiled at her. "I'm Ron."

"Don't tell her your name," his wife squealed.

Ron laughed and stood, still staring. Darlene saw with horror that he was getting hard. She didn't like the way he was looking her over.

Darlene raised the Desert Eagle and pointed it at his dick. "I'll be leaving now."

He was still holding the .357 loosely in his hand and in her general direction. "What if I asked you nicely to stay?"

"Sorry, but I think it's time for me to leave." Darlene took a step toward the door.

"You motherfucker, you think you're gonna put that dirty dick in this whore while I'm still alive?" the woman asked.

Ron ignored her and smiled again at Darlene, now fully erect.

Another step closer to the door and Darlene figured she was almost free of this nightmare scene. "I'm leaving," she said firmly.

"Why don't you stay? Safety in numbers, you know." He took a step closer but held the gun to his side. "The three of us could band together."

"I don't think so, Ronnie." The woman glanced at Darlene. "Not with her. No offense."

Darlene wanted to laugh. "None taken." She took another step sideways to the door. "Good luck to both of you."

Ron dropped the smile as he stared at Darlene's crotch. "You're not going anywhere."

"Ronnie, so help me God -"

The woman never finished her sentence before he turned on her and shot her in the chest.

Darlene reacted and pulled the trigger, the bullet slicing through his neck. She didn't wait to see who lived and died because she ran down the hallway, crashing into the wall and knocking family collages off as she went.

The back door was locked, she realized too late as she went crashing into it, but it didn't shatter. She heard one of them moaning from the bedroom. She turned, ready to shoot, but no one appeared. Reaching back blindly, she unlocked the door and stepped backwards into the cool morning.

She broke and ran for the side gate, which was open. Darlene started to run, getting six houses away before she stopped to catch her breath and push the fear down. The street was empty.

"What happened to the dog?" she whispered.

With no one in pursuit and no zombies in the immediate area she began a methodical search of the houses. She needed to find some clothing, food and more bullets.

Chapter Eight

Hitch A Ride

"The greatest song ever. Am I right?" R.J. didn't wait for an answer from Darlene. Instead he cranked the song - AC/DC's seminal *Highway To Hell* - and floored the Trans Am. He began warbling along completely out of tune.

Darlene closed her eyes and prayed that he wouldn't kill them both. Since 'meeting him' in the Wawa he'd been cordial, if a bit eccentric.

R.J. had a Jersey accent and crazy look in his eyes, but wore a cowboy hat, faded blue jeans and a huge Confederate flag belt buckle. He'd been punching the fountain drink machine to magically get it to work, even though the store had been ransacked and the power was off.

He'd made no move for a weapon and didn't seem fazed when she drew the Desert Eagle on him. Instead, he tipped his cowboy hat in her direction, winked, and asked if she knew how the soda machine worked.

"Yeah, I know how it works. With electricity," she replied sarcastically.

"None of that around here. I guess I'll mosey along to other parts of the range, eh?" he'd said but in a thick Joisey accent. Darlene thought it quite unsettling but he didn't seem to be a threat. After what she'd just escaped from...

She watched him warily but went about trying to find something to eat or drink.

"You won't find anything else in here, ma'am," he'd said. "Picked it clean and stored it in the Bandit outside."

"Bandit?"

He pumped out his chest and went to the broken glass windows at the front of the store and pointed. "I call her Bandit, like what Burt drove."

Outside, parked by itself, was a white Pontiac Trans Am.

"His was black," Darlene said matter-of-factly.

He grinned. "Well, no shit... sorry 'bout the language... I'll be painting it as soon as I get back home and making sure the gold eagle is touched up and fancy."

"Where's home?" She was waiting for some bullshit answer like Dallas or Oklahoma City.

"Swedesboro."

"Never heard of it," she admitted.

"South Jersey, nice and quiet. I just need to get back home and then I'll have time to paint my new car, wrangle up some horses, and plant some corn."

"Sounds like a plan." Darlene's stomach was growling. "Any chance you'd be willing to share some of your food with me? I haven't eaten in a few days."

"Need a ride? I could always use someone riding shotgun."

"Sure." Darlene didn't know what else to do, and she was getting sick and tired of walking. Two long weeks and she was still firmly inside New York State, and knew she'd been heading in an eastern direction due to zombies, road blocks, fires and hostile living people.

Now they were cranking tunes and driving way too fast.

"You said you had food," Darlene screamed over the guitar solo.

R.J. pointed a meaty finger behind him. "Grab whatever you want. The stuff is all over the place, but see if you can find me a beer. I should have a couple left."

She rummaged through some bags and found a warm can of cheap beer. "You probably shouldn't drink and drive," she said as she opened it for him. It was said as a joke but she was also concerned.

"Who's going to arrest me, the zombie police?"

"True." She found another beer and held that one for herself. "How bad are these cookies?"

"Stale as shit but still considered food."

"You know you have a bottle of wine?"

"Sweet. Bring it up, we'll cannonball it with the beers and get ripped."

She stuffed cookies in her mouth and washed it down with the warm beer. Not a bad meal when you hadn't eaten in days.

Darlene decided that she'd rather die drunk and full of stale cookies in a car crash than bitten and sexually abused by a dead person.

* * * * *

"Where are we?" she said, sitting up in the Trans Am. Her body was stiff. When she realized they were parked she slowly rolled out of the car and stretched her legs. It was nighttime.

R.J. tipped his hat. "Connecticut."

"I thought we were going to New Jersey."

"We are. But we can't very well swing through NYC and fight a zillion zombies, can we? Most of the roads were blocked off as we headed south so I had to turn west." He was siphoning gas from a pickup truck. "I'll fill 'er up and we'll be on our way."

"Did you search this place?"

"Nah, just stopped a few minutes ago and took a leak. You've been sleeping for about twelve hours."

"Maybe we should hide out until daybreak. It's probably not a good idea to drive at night, when you can't see far enough ahead."

"Agreed. Even with it being such a clear night, it was getting dicey there the last couple of hours. I just wanted to put some distance between us and that last city I skirted, because it was crawling with the dead. It looked like an ant swarm or cockroaches or something."

"Where are we?"

R.J. laughed. "In Connecticut. That's all I know."

They were parked right off an exit from a major highway in a strip-mall. The windows had all been smashed out, but nothing on fire. Darlene was thankful for that.

There was a pizza place, a hobby shop, a tanning salon, Chinese takeout, and a liquor store. "Finished with your wine?" she asked.

"Almost." R.J. finished filling the Trans Am. "Let me get my machete and we'll go look for something expensive. I prefer a white wine, if possible."

"Beggars can't be choosers," Darlene said. "We'll start at the end at the liquor store and work our way to some fine pizza."

The liquor store was open, all the glass doors and windows shattered. The shelves were empty, but they searched anyway.

"In every movie I ever saw about a zombie apocalypse, there is always a bottle of something for the heroes to find," R.J. said from behind the counter.

"Who says we're the heroes?"

"You think those things are the heroes? If that's the case, it means we're all fucked."

"We're fucked regardless." Darlene wished right now she had a flashlight, because scampering in the dark with glass everywhere was not a good move. Besides, she knew this was a bust.

"Did you hear that?" R.J. said at the same moment she heard the car engine.

* * * * *

"Two guys, ones big and looks like a biker, the other is small with glasses." Darlene leaned forward and watched the odd pair as they exited the beat-up station wagon.

"Are they heading our way?" R.J. asked.

"So far they're standing outside the car and whispering. I can't make out what they're saying." She turned to R.J. "I don't want to fight living people if I can help it. If they leave us alone I say we leave them alone."

"Sounds like a plan. The last time I ran into people they tried to shoot me and take the Bandit."

Darlene thought about the worst time she'd run into people and what they'd done to her, but she pushed it down, deep out of the way, before it consumed her again. No sense in dwelling on the past when the present was so fucked up.

They stayed in the shadows and waited. Finally, Darlene watched with relief as the two men pulled shotguns from the car but went into the hobby store a couple storefronts away.

When she told R.J. he nodded. "We wait them out."

Darlene was fine with that. Within ten minutes the duo reappeared, lugging large white boxes. "What did they find?"

R.J. took a peek and chuckled. "They're taking the comic books and baseball cards."

"Seriously?"

"Looks like it. Shit, if that place went untouched they might be in there for a couple hours between searching and loading up the station wagon."

"Great." Darlene wondered if there was someplace comfortable to crash in here until then.

"We need to leave," R.J. said suddenly.

"I think we just sit tight and the geeks will be gone stealing Iron Man comic books in a few. Then we can drive out of here."

R.J. began wringing his hands. "I need to get home."

"All in good time. Don't start freaking out," Darlene said. She casually moved away from him, making pretend she was looking for something they might have missed. "Did we check the stockroom?"

R.J. seemed to relax. "I'll do that. You keep an eye on those two."

Darlene hoped it would keep him busy and preoccupied until these guys left.

They were carrying out another two boxes and adding them to the back of the station wagon. She wondered what would possess them to take items that were worthless.

She could see loading up the car with boxes of canned food or gallons and gallons of water, but cards and comics didn't make sense.

Then again, what really did make sense these days? Dead people eating living people was pretty much out there in space as well. It felt like all the rules had changed, and you survived and that was the bottom line.

Darlene sat in the shadows near the front window and watched as the two continued bringing out their finds. She wondered what they'd been like before this happened. It was a safe assumption they'd been heavily into comic books and video games.

She remembered an old *Saturday Night Live* skit from years ago when William Shatner was at a Star Trek convention and he asked one of the geeky kids if he'd ever kissed a girl. Darlene wondered if either of them had, but with her luck they were more than likely psycho rapists. At this point, based on who'd she'd met so far in her journey, three out of four guys were horny serial killers.

For a second she just stared blankly when she saw the brake lights of the Bandit flash. By the time she stood and went to the doorway the car was driving away.

When the two guys came out, shotguns drawn, she faded back into the store and held the Desert Eagle.

"Dumb wannabe hillbilly," she whispered.

The Trans Am shot out of the parking lot before he turned the headlights on.

After a minute the two guys went back inside to complete their mission.

Chapter Nine

Lords of the Flies

Darlene Bobich, feet tired and down to her last can of corn, rested against a wall of the Havenwood High School. She felt like she'd been walking for days, because she had.

When R.J. ran off with the Bandit (the Pontiac Trans Am) and left her she was furious. That anger sustained her for the first couple of hours on the walk, but now she'd wash his damn car if he pulled up and offered her a lift.

She was skirting the New York - Connecticut border, slipping in and out of small towns while she moved. But she didn't find much. It seemed like a great horde were just over the next ridge, pillaging the houses and stores a mile ahead of her and clearing them out.

Living and undead were in scarce supply and at least that was something to be grateful for. She knew the school might not offer a comfortable resting place but it might offer some shelter, especially if she could hide in one of the classrooms and sleep.

Maybe a teacher hid some candy bars or an energy drink in their desk, she thought. At this point she'd be happy with stale crumbs in the bottom of an empty potato chip bag.

As she got the strength to move again a strangled cry sounded from just around the building. Darlene led with the Desert Eagle.

The girl looked to be no more than ten, with curly blonde hair and wearing a light blue dress. She sat on top of a picnic table in the enclosed courtyard, hands in her lap.

Darlene stopped short and lowered her weapon.

The girl smiled at her. "Hi," she said, as if they'd met in a store or restaurant. "My name is Stephanie."

"I'm Darlene. Honey, what are you doing out here alone?" Darlene moved slowly toward her. The girl was clearly living and she didn't seem to be bleeding or have any noticeable bite marks. "Do you know how dangerous this is?"

The girl, still smiling, nodded and kept her eyes locked on Darlene's without blinking. It was unnerving.

"Freeze."

Darlene was too late to react when she felt the muzzle pushed against her side.

"Move a muscle and I'll shoot you, lady."

Darlene slowly raised her hands but kept the Desert Eagle. She turned her head slightly and looked. The shotgun ended in a boy, maybe twelve, with reddish hair and freckles. Behind him were seven or eight other kids, all wielding baseball bats, hockey sticks or steel bars. "I don't want any trouble," she said.

"Too late. This is our territory, lady."

"I understand. I'm going to turn around and walk out of here and no one will get hurt."

"If you take one step I'll fill you full of lead," the boy said.

Darlene wanted to laugh at the cliché he'd just said, and every other one he'd make before this was over. *Too much TV watching for this kid*, Darlene thought.

"Kid, where are your parents?" As soon as she said it she cringed. Of *all the stupid things to say*. "I mean, who's in charge here? You?"

He pushed the shotgun into her side, harder, and nodded. "I'm in charge here. This is my school and my playground and my town. You're trespassing. Do you know what we do with trespassers?"

Darlene shook her head, casually glancing at the other children. They hung on his every word, fear, awe and hunger clearly etched on their faces.

"We gut them and eat them."

"Bobby, don't say that. I'm not eating anyone," Stephanie said. "You wanted to lure the monsters in so we could kill them. She's not a monster."

"I make that decision, not you."

"Who said you were the leader of us, anyway?" another boy said. "You're only calling the shots because you have your dad's rifle."

"Don't challenge me, Brent, or I'll kick your ass."

"You can try," Brent said.

Darlene knew this would quickly escalate into in-fighting, with someone likely to get hurt. She didn't want any part of this, especially with kids involved. If Bobby accidentally pulled that trigger or turned the gun on the group and fired she didn't know if she could live with that. "After all I've been through, kids killing kids would suck," she whispered.

Bobby turned his attention back to her. "What did you say?"

"I said you and I need to talk."

Bobby smiled but Darlene could see he was scared. The muzzle brushed against her side but he couldn't hold it steady. "There's nothing to talk about. I'm in charge and I call the shots." Darlene watched in horror as his fingers kept flexing on the trigger.

"You do know that shotgun wouldn't do anything to me at this close range?"

Bobby looked down at the weapon, which was what Darlene was hoping for. She pushed it aside and had her Desert Eagle out and pointed at his chest.

The group scattered.

"That just broke my heart to put a gun to a child. But, Bobby, this standoff needs to end right now. I need to leave."

He nodded his head, tears starting to form. "I'm just scared."

"I know you are." Darlene took a step back and lowered the gun but reached out and grabbed the shotgun from his limp fingers. "We all are."

"Not you."

"I'm pissing my pants, Bobby."

He laughed at her joke and wiped at his face. "Stay with us, be our leader."

"How about you all come with me? I'm heading south before the winter comes."

"We live here. This is all I know and the rest. Besides, my parents are here somewhere. When this all started my mom drove out to get my grandma and my dad was on his way from work. I need to stay close to my house and take care of my sister."

Darlene nodded. "But you're a bunch of kids."

Bobby laughed. "A bunch of kids that have survived this long. We have a house full of food and water, and we built a tunnel. That's the only way into the garage now."

"I can't just leave you."

"It looks like we're doing better than you. When was the last time you ate something?"

"True."

Bobby called for Stephanie, who came running. Darlene put her Desert Eagle back in her waistband. "Sis, go get this lady something to eat from the house, and some water. Take Jimmy with you."

"I can't cut into your supplies like that," Darlene said.

"Just through the woods there is a shopping center. We cleared out all the food from the big store and all the small ones. We have three rooms packed with food."

"Thank you." Darlene said. "Sure you don't want to come?"

"We're fine here. These are my friends and they look up to me."

"You're a natural born leader, Bobby."

Darlene went and sat down on the picnic table. She was about to leave a group of little kids alone, to fend for themselves, during such trying times.

"All the rules have changed," she whispered and smiled when Stephanie approached with an opened can of corn.

Chapter Ten

Rear Guard

Darlene Bobich knew the fallacy in Barry's statement.

"The living leave a heat signature, and I can easily pick it up with my scope. If they're cold as, well, a fucking dead person, I blow their fucking head off. Case closed."

"Recently deceased people still have a small amount of heat."

"Nah." Barry dismissed her with a wave of his hand as he scanned the highway behind them. "They die and the heat goes with them. It only takes a few minutes. My daddy was a doctor, trust me."

"Your daddy was a doctor?" Darlene asked skeptically.

Barry winked at her. "He was a janitor in the state hospital in Rhode Island. Same thing. He knew stuff."

"By that logic I'm a five star general." Darlene held up her Desert Eagle semi-automatic. "I know how to shoot a gun at things."

"Now we're getting somewhere." Barry wiped the sweat from his forehead. Even in his early sixties, Barry had more energy than most of the people she'd met. His wiry gray beard stopped right below his large ears, his head bald and sunburned. A single diamond earring in his left ear was his only jewelry, his clothes nondescript. He wore over-sized work boots and carried a hunting rifle with his bedroll and supplies tied to his back. A Beretta PX4 was always in his hands.

They'd been moving steadily south for three days, with Barry and Darlene part of the Rear Guard. Six groups of two were spread out across a half-mile line, and the occasional sound of a weapon discharging had become so common that no one bothered to investigate unless signaled.

Darlene was the only female in the Rear Guard and only because she was one of the few females that had a weapon and knew how to use it. It was better than being on the Death Squad or on the Scavengers.

"It will be light soon," Darlene said. She didn't know if the nights or the days were worse; at night the undead would enter their flashlight range from out of the blackness, rotting limbs and gore-streaked clothing. The males were the worst, with engorged dicks and wagging tongues. During the day it was easier to see them, but it was easier to see how many followed the group. Sometimes the road took them past a large metropolis and hundreds of the former residents would get in behind them.

Barry estimated that they'd been leading over twenty thousand behind them at this point, shuffling slowly from New Haven, Connecticut to their present location just south of Baltimore. It was pretty impressive when you considered that they currently had about two hundred living people in their makeshift caravan. The odds were against them.

"We need to get moving a bit faster," Barry said loudly. The rear walkers of their group were right behind them, the slow and the weak stragglers. Several times each night they would be yelled at, pushed and cajoled or risk behind left behind.

Darlene was reminded of the ambush in Weehawken in Jersey about ten nights ago, when scores of undead came from all sides and wedged them into a parking lot, where they used too much ammunition and lost too many living to escape. Most of the 'back group' had been sacrificed, torn to pieces as the healthier broke free and got away.

It seemed like every few miles another two or three living would hear them coming, see the spotlights from the trucks, buses and cars and join them, bringing whatever food and weapons they had.

There was no organization. Six military men, still in uniform and using their Army lingo and hand signals, were trying to lead the group toward an unspecified rendezvous point due south. Darlene hadn't bothered to speak with them personally. They seemed either too shell-shocked or too arrogant to deal with.

Barry had been to the front of the group each day to get the same orders as the last: guard the rear, shoot the undead and keep people moving. So far they'd done a serviceable job of it.

Darlene had been in the group about three weeks, hooking up with them just outside of the Connecticut/New York border. At first she'd followed at a safe distance. The last large group she'd encountered before that had been in Buffalo, a militia faction from upstate that had taken the apocalypse as reason to kill the living and the undead. She'd escaped with her life and only a few bruises.

"Incoming," Barry said.

Three silhouettes appeared just beyond flashlight range. "Living," Jonathan shouted from their left. He was in his late teens, a gangly kid with glasses and a few wisps of a moustache. He'd been the first person to befriend Darlene and to recommend her for the Rear Guard.

They stopped and watched warily as the three approached. Lately the living were presenting problems as well, with beggars and thieves latching onto them. Two nights ago a man, who everyone thought had been paralyzed from his waist down in an attack and who rode on the back of one of the pickups, tried to highjack the truck with a box cutter. He had perfect use of his legs, running away when his robbery was thwarted.

One of the military men had put a bullet cleanly through the back of his head at fifty paces and they'd left the body.

"Hands where I can see them," Barry said. When they got to within ten feet he stopped them with a raised hand. "How can we help you?"

The three were filthy. Darlene could smell the rot from where she stood, gun trained on the oldest one's head. It seemed to her that the survivors were getting sorrier by the day.

"We need help, that's all, some food and safety. I'm Russ." He held his hands up and tried to smile. "We just need help." Darlene thought he was in his late forties but it was hard to tell with all the dirt caked on his face and clothes.

"This is Tiff, she's my daughter." The girl looked to be around Jonathan's age. She was looking down at her feet and her hands were shaking. Her dress had been torn and besides mud she had streams of dried blood coating it.

Russ turned to the third member of his party, another man covered in muck. "I'm sorry, I can't remember what your name –"

Jonathan shot the girl between the eyes.

It took several seconds for Darlene to register what had happened. Russ wailed and fell upon his daughter's body while the Rear Guard took a step or three back, guns before them.

"Did you smell her?" Jonathan asked.

"You did well. Believe me, you did well," Barry said. "She was ripe and she would have been dead soon enough."

Russ stood, tears streaking his dirty face, and made an angry lunge toward Jonathan. Darlene put her pistol to the man's head. "She was dying and you know it."

"She was getting better; we just needed food and rest. And you killed her."

"She would have killed you," Darlene whispered.

Russ turned his eyes to Darlene. "She was my daughter."

"In a couple of hours she would have been like all the rest, and she would have killed you and everyone here if we'd have let you join us."

Russ fell to his knees. "She was the reason I was alive, she saved me back there. She saved her father's life." He started to cry again.

Darlene pointed her gun at the third member of their group. "What's your story?"

The man audibly gulped. "I'm Daniel. I'm just in need of some food, looking to join you guys and get to safety. I just met them yesterday and stayed away from her when she got bit, I swear. I have a .357 in my right pocket with three bullets left. I was planning on using one on her if I had to." He smiled and nodded at Jonathan. "You saved me a bullet."

Barry nudged Russ with the toe of his work boot. "What now?"

Russ looked up at him. "What do you mean?"

Barry glanced over his shoulder. "While we've been here talking the group has moved off, too far for comfort. If anything is around they've heard the gunshot and are on their way to eat us. We need to move right now."

"Okay." Russ wiped his eyes with a filthy sleeve and bent to pick up his daughter.

"I don't think so." Barry gripped the man by his arm. "She's been infected, and we don't know if it spreads any other way besides the biting and the, uh, other ways. Besides, we only have a few pickups and trucks and we use them to catch an hour or two of sleep. Space is limited; we can't carry the dead with us."

"I won't leave her."

"That's your prerogative," Barry said and turned away. "Good luck."

The Rear Guard jogged to catch back up with the group, Daniel in with them.

Darlene hoped that the man came to his senses and left the body, but she doubted he would. More than likely he'd be overrun by zombies and they'd rip him apart before starting on her corpse. She supposed it was better that it was still dark. She'd only be able to hear his screams. Eventually, during a rest stop, father and daughter would catch up to them and Barry would blast them both between the eyes. It never failed.

The newest member, Daniel, moved forward to see if he could be useful while the Rear Guard continued to patrol and scan the horizon for undead.

An hour later they were relieved, and they climbed onto a nearby pickup truck and spread out as much as possible. Darlene, Barry and Jonathan were joined by five others, who Darlene knew by face but not by name.

"Another day, another death," Barry said. He rubbed his bald head and then his eyes. "I hope I can sleep."

"I wish I could sleep with my eyes open. Closing them shows me too many bad things." Jonathan leaned his head against the side of the truck. "I wonder if the Scavengers found any food. I can't remember the last time I ate."

"I can't remember the last time I had a decent meal," Darlene said.

"I can. It was at McCoy Stadium in Pawtucket. Two Monster Dogs, cheese fries and three draft beers." Barry closed his eyes and grinned. "I'd give my left nut for a Monster Dog right now."

"Gross," Darlene said but laughed. "I'd give anything for a nice Maine lobster right now."

"You from Maine?" Barry asked.

"Born and bred. Just outside of Dexter." Darlene patted her Desert Eagle. "My daddy actually made this pistol in the factory and bought it for me and trained me on its proper use."

"Touching," Jonathan said. Everyone laughed.

"Anyone have any idea how this shit started?" a woman asked. She was fit and in her thirties but only wore dirty ripped jeans and a soiled bra. This was the first time Darlene had heard her speak even though some shifts they walked a few paces apart on Rear Guard. Darlene had no idea what her name was.

"That voodoo guy in Montreal who killed his kids," someone said.

"Nah, it was the oil spill in the Gulf that brought up those black creatures, I saw it on CNN right before the TV went out."

"I know for a fact it was because that pilot in Alaska crashed and had to eat his wife and son. It was like mad cow disease."

"It's because we've pissed off God and he's purging the earth of the sinners."

"Hell was full."

"I saw that story about the chick with O.C.D. and she swears when she stopped counting shit this shit happened."

"Some crazy fucker had sex with a green monkey and instead of another strain of AIDS in created undead."

Darlene curled up and closed her eyes. "Good night, my friends." No one knew the real reason and she didn't want to hear another thirty conjectures before she slept.

"Night," Barry said, followed by the rest.

Her dreams were troubled but she woke a few hours later and couldn't remember them. She was always thankful for that. They'd all gotten used to the rough ride on the back of the trucks and flatbeds, sneaking as many winks as possible before going back to their job.

"Where's Jonathan?" Darlene asked Barry. He was already sitting on the tailgate of the truck watching the sun creep slowly on the horizon.

"Military guy came by about an hour ago. Jonathan was awake so they recruited him."

"For what?"

The pickup stopped and everyone shook off their meager sleep and hit the ground.

"We're running short of everything again, especially fuel. There is a library a block or two over and it looks intact." Barry pointed at the road they'd come from. "There's a huge mass of the dead about a mile behind us, maybe a thousand. We're moving way too slow to outdistance them, so we might try to hole up and let them pass."

Darlene slapped the side of the pickup truck and it stopped. They hopped off the back and immediately followed along with everyone else, a stream of bodies heading through a convenience store parking lot.

Two men carrying baseball bats stood outside the shattered store. "It's already been picked clean," one of them said to Darlene when she looked their way.

"She does have a great ass," the other man said to his partner, loud enough for Darlene to hear. She ignored it. She'd seen enough sexual violence in the last month or so, either done to her or by the undead to others, to last a lifetime and to keep her dreams filled with terror and death. The last thing she needed was sex. "Who are you trying to kid?" she whispered. Without trying to seem obvious she glanced back at the man to see what he looked like. He was handsome, rugged and dirty like everyone else. He was also smiling and staring at her. She turned away.

"Let's get the hurt inside," someone kept shouting over and over from the steps of the library, a small building with glass windows. As she stopped on the steps to let people file past her she could already see the efficiency of the group: wooden boards were being used as covering on the windows, both shattered and intact, while three men were dragging the tables and chairs outside to use as kindling or for the defenses. An older woman began whittling on a chair leg with a pocketknife.

One of the military men approached her. "You Death Squad?"

"Rear Guard."

"You're Death Squad now." He pointed to a sickly old man sitting on the back of a pickup truck. "Take him over to the next block and take care of it. He won't last another hour."

Darlene swallowed hard. "I'm Rear Guard."

"Right now you're helping all of us to stay alive by taking dying people and shooting them in the head." He eyed her. "Do it."

"Sir, yes sir," she said sarcastically but he was already turned away from her. Darlene went to the back of the pickup truck. The man was in bad condition, with a plethora of cuts and bruises. His thumb was sheared from his left hand and it was wrapped in a dirty shirt, a bandage around his head, blood seeping through the soiled cloth from his eye socket.

"I need some help," Darlene said to the driver as he got out of the truck.

He smiled and shook his head. "I'm just the driver, I ain't the Death Squad."

"Dickhead."

"Bitch."

Darlene closed her eyes and rubbed her temples. This day was getting worse and worse. The prospect of holing up in a library with a roof over her head and perhaps some food and water kept her going. "Hurry up, bitch, and get this done so we can relax for a bit," she whispered.

"Let's go." She helped him off of the truck.

The fear was plainly sketched on his face.

"I can do this, I have to do this," she whispered. She tried not to look at him again, preferring to ignore the fact that she'd have to kill an innocent person before he died and tried to kill her. It didn't make it any easier. She took the Desert Eagle out and held it low as they moved.

A block away they stopped. "I'm sorry," was all she could muster. Darlene had begun to cry at some point.

"Let me go," he said. "My name is Paul. What's your name?"

Darlene shook her head. "No names."

"I promise I'll get as far away as possible, clear across this city."

Darlene hesitated. *How far could he really get on his own before he died or was attacked and turned into a zombie?* "I can't."

"You can, you can. Does it make a difference if we're killed out there or by another living person's hand at this point? Can you have that on your conscience? I know I couldn't kill another human being." The old man shifted on his feet. "Turn away and we'll be gone."

"I can't risk that. What if you died and came back and killed me? Remembered me or where we were hiding?"

"Do you really think those mindless things can do that?"

"I don't know. I can't take a chance." Darlene held the gun at eye level. "I can't. I'm sorry."

"But you can," Paul pleaded falling roughly to one knee and folding his hands together in prayer. "You're better than this, I know you are."

Darlene tried to keep her hand steady as she held the pistol. She needed one clean shot to his head to end it, and her violent shaking might force her to shoot him a second or third time before he died. She didn't want to pull the trigger once, let alone another.

"You're good people, raised right, I know you are," Paul was saying, words rushing out of his mouth now as he pleaded for his life. "I'm fine, I feel better, and I could walk back with you to the library or help you find us some food and water. I could be your servant, yes, I could, help you with your patrols and watch over you while you sleep." Paul tried to stifle a coughing fit.

"I can't. Stop talking." Darlene lowered the weapon and rubbed her temple with her free hand.

"I have a wife out there, and grandchildren." Paul stood slowly. "I have pictures of the grandchildren in my wallet, let me show you little Michael."

One moment the old man was standing there, trying desperately to look fit and trim despite the fact that his feet kept buckling under and his many cuts were bleeding. The next his head shattered, spitting gore and crimson and death several feet in any direction.

Darlene moved by instinct, the last weeks of running taking her over the edge and beyond. Before she could catch her breath or blink she'd already lifted the Desert Eagle and pulled the trigger twice to her immediate right.

"Oh my God." She went to Jonathan just as he fell, his .357 slipping from his grip. His eyes were wide and unseeing, two bloody holes growing on his chest.

Jonathan had come out of nowhere when he'd shot the old man. "Why didn't you say something? Why not show yourself before doing that?"

Darlene cradled his head and sobbed. She considered him one of her only friends. Besides Barry she was alone, with no one to guard her back. Despite the age difference between them she thought they had a lot in common, and kept each other grounded.

"Where were you from?" Darlene whispered, ashamed that she'd spent so much time with this kid and couldn't remember too many personal details about his life before everything turned upside down. "Did you have two loving parents? A job? A girlfriend?"

For the first time in weeks the world around her simply stopped; all sound shut out from her. She welcomed it, wondering if she had somehow died as well and was at peace. *If I died right now, would I be at rest, or would I still be in this shell, shuffling along with my killer, trying to kill others?* Darlene didn't care to know the answer. She hoped that death would be the end, period, take me to Heaven and let me in moment. With death so close at every step, either through zombie attacks, lack of food and water, dehydration, no medicine, crazy militia and marauders and looters, or simply falling into a ditch and never being found…

It didn't register at first that Jonathan had opened his eyes and his mouth as she sat with him on the ground cupping his head gently.

"I'm sorry," she whispered. She stroked his hair, oblivious to the fact that he was squirming under her weight.

"All I wanted was a friend, someone to talk to, someone to share stories with, and someone to laugh at my jokes. Does that sound cliché to you?"

"Very cliché, to be honest," Barry said as he pulled Darlene forcefully up off of the ground and put his booted foot on the chest of their former friend. "But now I know why I'm in love with you, Darlene Bobich."

Barry shot Jonathan in the face at pointblank range, covering Darlene's dirty pants in blood. They watched as the lifeless body of their friend slumped on the ground.

"We need to go, they're all around us," Barry said.

Darlene stood numbly, staring at the body. *When will this end? When will the death stop finding us?*

"This way." Barry dragged her to the side of a building just as a dozen undead came into view. "They've cut us off from the library. Shit."

Darlene shook off the depression and followed Barry around the corner and through a ripped chain-link fence. They stopped when three zombies barred their path to the next street.

"Now what?" Barry asked.

"In here," Darlene said and kicked open the nearest door. They plunged inside and did their best to shut the splintered door. Barry produced a flashlight and lit up the room. For a second the beam lingered on a figure sprawled on the ground and they thought they had company, but it was an actual dead person.

"Help me with this." Barry grabbed one end of a couch and they slid it across the floor and against the doorway, then piled as much furniture as they could find onto it. The two windows were still intact but easily broken. Shapes moved outside.

Without a word they ascended the steps to the second floor. At the top of the stairs they entered a dark hall with three closed doors before them.

"Which one?" Darlene asked.

As if in answer the nearest door burst open and two undead fought around one another to attack. Barry shot one in the head at pointblank range. The other gripped his arm.

Darlene shot him twice in the face and kicked him away as he fell. Barry slumped against the wall.

"So much for hiding up here and hoping they pass us by." Darlene slowly entered the room with her Desert Eagle drawn before her. She gasped.

Another zombie was kneeling before them, his head buried in the V of a woman's crotch, blood and pus running on the carpet. The zombie looked up, pieces of flesh dripping from its mouth.

Darlene shot it three times in the head until her pistol was out of ammo. She turned away, closed the door and searched her pockets for more ammo.

The farthest room down the hall was empty save for some overturned furniture. Barry went to the window and glanced out. "They're everywhere. If we stay quiet maybe they'll pass us by."

They could hear banging outside and below them and the sound of glass shattering. They piled the chairs and bed frame against the door.

"I don't want to die today," Barry murmured to himself.

Darlene loaded her weapon and crouched next to the window. She held her breath as the banging below them stopped. "You hear that?" she whispered.

Gunfire was clearly heard in the direction of the library. She wondered how they were faring. In the short time she'd been in the group she'd met a few nice people, survivors looking to help one another and face the unknown as a team. She envied the older ones and the mothers protecting their children, people who had lost their loved ones: husbands, wives, children, parents, friends and neighbors.

"This might be our last day," Barry said from behind her. "There's pretty much no chance of us getting out of here alive now. They've caught up with us. There might be a million of them out there."

"Keep quiet." Darlene watched as the streets flooded with undead, and the stench of their rot wafted up to her. She fought the urge to gag on what little she'd eaten. "If we stay here for a few hours we might escape." She didn't want to think about the rest of the group. More than likely, by the sound of gunfire and the screams that now echoed outside, her former friends would soon become her enemies.

"I've been putting together a bucket list in my head lately, all the things I want to do before I die."

Darlene shushed him to be quiet without looking at Barry. He was getting annoying now. Couldn't he shut the fuck up before the sound brought them?

"Guess what my top slot is?"

Darlene brushed something off of her shoulder. At first she thought it was Barry's hand or a bug, but when she turned her head she was staring straight at Barry's engorged dick. "What the fuck?" she stammered.

"Exactly. I want to fuck you before I die. I have since the moment I saw you."

"Barry, get the fuck away from me." Darlene stood but Barry, standing in the buff and now stroking his cock, had blocked her into the corner next to the window.

"You know you want this as much as I do."

"I'm going to count to three and then I'll scream."

Barry laughed. "And give away our position to them? I don't think so. Besides, we might as well have some fun in case they catch us. If they pass us by, so much the better."

"I'm warning you."

Barry was on her in a rush, hands wrapping around her and squeezing her ass fiercely. His tongue darted around her neck area and he was moaning.

She tried with all of her might to push him off but he was too strong despite his smaller stature. His fingers dug into the back of her jeans and he was trying to rip them off of her.

They slammed against the window, jarring the glass. Her jeans had come undone and Barry dragged them down her thighs.

Darlene punched frantically at him but her blows were ineffective. Her vision blurred as she remembered the attack from the militia and how brutal they had been to her. At some point she'd started crying.

"I knew you had thongs on," Barry was whispering in her ear now, drool sliding from his lips and coating her cheek. "I am gonna tear that little ass of yours up."

He slid a finger under her undies and tried to bury the digit inside her.

Barry was still smiling as Darlene jammed the Desert Eagle into his stomach and pulled the trigger. His eyes grew wide in shock but he didn't let go. "I loved you," he whispered before falling backwards.

Darlene kicked his body in the ribs before shooting him in the face four times.

She heard the pounding from below again and knew there was no escape. Resigned to that fact, she put her jeans back up as best she could and stared at the blocked door, the Desert Eagle ready to fire.

Chapter Eleven

Undead of Winter

A weak ray of light woke her from a restless sleep. She immediately gripped the gun and scanned the room with it. Empty.

"What the fuck happened?" Darlene whispered. The furniture was still pushed up against the door, although a chair had toppled at some point. Barry was still on the floor, blood and guts coagulating and reeking. A hundred flies had settled on the crimson mess of his remains.

Slowly, she walked across the room and removed a chair. She placed an ear to the door but heard nothing. "Don't open the door," she muttered. In every horror movie she'd ever watched, the stupid bitch female had opens the door and gets decapitated with a machete or has her throat slit.

Instead, she went to the window and looked to the street below. It was empty of living and dead. There was blood on everything, though, and she knew while she'd slept another war had been waged. She didn't know who won.

Darlene suddenly remembered the large group she'd been traveling with: two hundred strong, moving from Connecticut to here, near Baltimore. Yesterday – or earlier today? – they'd holed up in a library, but Darlene was assigned Death Squad duty to kill a sickly member of the group. In addition, she'd managed to kill Jonathan and, later, Barry. Barry deserved it, having tried to rape her while they hid. Jonathan had been a good kid. A young kid just trying to survive like everyone else.

"Fuck it," she whispered. For some reason, since the world had gone to Hell, she'd whispered her thoughts. Ironically, there was no one living to hear her words. Like now.

Going back to the door, she slowly pulled the piled-up furniture away from in front of it and gripped the handle. She held the gun at the ready and turned the knob. Before pulling the door open, she got into a shooting stance, wiped sweat from her face with a dirty sleeve and tried in vain to relax her body. Far from ideal conditions to kill anything on the other side of the door, she really didn't have a choice.

Darlene tugged the door open and came within a fraction of a second of pulling the trigger at an empty hallway. "Fuck." Instead of a pile of body parts or a horde of zombies waiting patiently to kill her, there was nothing. Gouges in the doorframe shocked her. She was amazed the door had held.

She went to the end of the hallway, glancing into open doors and ignoring the closed ones – no sense in opening one and having it squeak and alert the undead – and went down the steps one at a time, as gingerly as possible.

Out on the street, she sniffed the cool morning air. When the dead were close you could usually smell them coming for blocks. Now she smelled smoke and nothing else.

The library, where the group was holed up, was two long blocks away. She figured she had three shots left in the Desert Eagle before she'd need to find ammo and knew how bad her odds were of doing it. Before the day ended, she'd need to find another weapon.

"And clothes," she whispered. She glanced down at the blood and dirt caked on her outfit. Her thong undies had been pulled and stretched in the fight with Barry and they rode uncomfortably in her ass crack. Her bra had been damaged, and under her shirt it kept slipping off her chest. She wished she had time to slip out of her undergarments or find new ones, but she wanted to feel safe first before getting naked. Stupid, she knew.

It was eerily quiet. The major cities had long ago been abandoned by the living and it seemed like the zombies followed their prey into the suburbs and the woods. But the cities still held more than enough of the undead.

She approached the caravan of vehicles they'd driven into town with the day before. None of them had been touched, which meant no fighting had occurred on the street in front of the library and there were no living scavengers in the immediate area; or maybe the undead were still teeming and no one was stupid enough to chance it.

Darlene wiped the sweat from her eyes and tried unsuccessfully to adjust her bra. Her thong was definitely digging into her and she'd probably chafe between that and the grime and the sweat. She'd give anything for a decent shower and some shampoo and soap right now.

Two dead bodies, sans heads, were wrapped together in a grotesque human sculpture on the steps of the library. The sun gleamed off the crimson coating they wore across their ravaged limbs and torsos. Darlene forced herself to look away.

The front doors to the library had been ruptured, blood and body parts covering the entryway. Darlene hesitated before entering the dark interior. Without a flashlight she would be blind. "Fuck it." She moved quickly and was glad to see the main area was well-lit by skylights. Unfortunately, it also allowed her to see the chaos and destruction that had ensued.

Pieces of bodies lay everywhere, the bookshelves and chairs were coated in crimson. No one moved, and not one body she could see was intact. She thanked God for that. She didn't know if she had the strength right now to fight a horde of undead in this closed space. A spiral staircase ran up on either side of the doors to a second tier, where more death covered the walls and books. She wanted to shout out for survivors but knew how stupid that would be. She doubted there were any.

She stepped gingerly across the room, trying to keep her breathing even and ignoring shadows on the walls. The last thing she wanted to do was waste bullets on nothing and alert the undead that she was here.

In the back of the library, down a narrow hall, Darlene came across a ransacked set of vending machines. Candy bars littered the ground and the soda machine had been jarred open. She grabbed three Snickers bars and ate them, then slowly opened the bathroom doors with her Desert Eagle leading the way. They were empty.

After washing down her food with two diet Cokes, Darlene cleaned her face in the ladies' room and intentionally didn't look at her reflection in the cracked mirror. Back in the hallway, she filled her pockets with candy and drank another soda.

The rear entrance to the library led into a parking lot that was now reduced to a riot of twisted metal cars and body parts. The fencing around the perimeter was intact but the gates had been ripped off and bent at odd angles, and a torched Honda Civic blocked the entrance.

Before Darlene could think, she ducked back behind the doors. Something moved out there, past the fences and the cars, and she was sure it wasn't alive.

Tears came to her eyes again and she decided to not be a hero and not try to figure out this puzzle just yet. She needed rest, real food, and for her hands to stop shaking. She closed the door and made sure it locked.

The front entrance wouldn't be so simple to secure. Darlene doubted she could close the doors enough or had the strength to push the heavy library furniture over to block it.

Back in the main room, nothing had been disturbed and nothing had entered while she was checking the rest of the building. She was thankful for that. One of the few military men left in the group, his head missing, was draped over a table. She went to him and pulled his M9 pistol from his dead fingers and found three detachable 15-round staggered box magazines – all full – in his pockets. She wondered why he still had so much ammo, but didn't complain. She'd been expecting to find two or three shells in the gun and nothing more.

Darlene was about to do a thorough search of the room when she heard something slam against one of the vehicles outside. She knew it was time to find a safe haven.

Upstairs, past gore and the stench of death, a utility closet with an intact door was her best bet. She tried her best to jam a broom handle against the door knob and put her back to the farthest wall. A small window told her she had a long wait until night fall, but she didn't care. She needed sleep and she needed to gather her strength. Who knew what tomorrow would bring?

* * * * *

A residential area netted Darlene quiet a catch: two apple trees, an orange tree and a working well with an old-fashioned hand pump. Despite the impending cold the fruit was still edible. It was a bit of a distance, but she'd been lucky enough to not run into too many of the undead in the two months she'd been living in the library.

The front doors had been sealed, the windows boarded up, and the back parking lot's gate mended enough to keep the undead out but still allow her to slip in and out. From the roof of the building, she could see all around her, and from there plan her next moves.

The highway she'd come in from was teeming with zombies, and in all directions she could see roaming packs of them. Fires and occasional explosions surrounded her, but she'd not seen another living person in weeks.

Settling into her hard wooden chair on the roof, she snuggled with two wool blankets and bit into an apple. The sun was dropping, and it was already cold. Baltimore didn't get as cold as Maine, but it was still going to be a bitter winter. Eventually she'd have to start a fire to keep warm and hope it wouldn't attract the undead or the living.

"Where am I going and what am I doing?" she whispered, tossing the apple in her hand. She didn't want to stay here through the winter, but now realized she should have done something about it weeks ago. It was just easier to stay where she was, in the relative safety of her library-fortress, and hope the world would go back to normal.

Darlene had been running for so long she was growing restless. She missed her home and she missed her father. At the thought of him, once again seeing him as he was before she pulled the trigger of the Desert Eagle, she started to cry. She knew Maine held nothing for her anymore, yet she longed to be there. By now her home had been ransacked and destroyed, her hometown of Dexter in ruins and aflame like here, but she didn't care. She needed to be somewhere, anywhere, but here. She knew how silly it sounded, and unrealistic.

The wind kicked up and she decided to go back inside.

* * * * *

The first flurries arrived a week later, while Darlene was raiding a diner, fighting the cockroaches for scraps of food. She'd found cans of tomato paste as well as two industrial cans of coffee.

It was while she was leaving through the hole that she'd entered through that she saw the movement across the street. She ducked down and peeked over the jagged edge, expecting to see a dozen zombies shambling towards her. Instead she saw a living, breathing person disappear into the darkness of the automotive store.

Snow fell on her face and hands, steaming away as she moved quietly across the desolate street. A quick check in both directions for zombies and then she was at the door, staring into the gloom.

She listened for any small noise to see where he'd gone but heard nothing. He was good, and that was probably why he was still alive. Eventually, her eyes adjusted and she was glad, because directly in front of her the floor had collapsed. She skirted to her left and followed around behind the counter, which had been picked clean.

Very rarely did she find anything of value anymore. The few survivors usually grabbed anything not bolted down, and unbolted what they could as well. At one point the store had been on fire, and the acrid smell still lingered in the cold air.

Darlene moved through the store with ease, noting the path she followed. It was well-worn and recent. This guy is smart. He has an escape route through this building, so he probably lives nearby.

The door to the back room was ajar and Darlene peered inside. The walls had been blown out and opened to the sky. She could see the snow had increased in the few minutes she'd been inside. It was still too warm to stick, but it would be soon enough.

Behind the store was a parking lot similar to the one at the library. The gates had been reinforced with car husks and a pile of office furniture, the surrounding buildings natural barriers.

There was only one door still intact and that was to the movie theatre in front of her. She went to the door and tried it, but it was locked. She smiled. The undead didn't try to turn knobs, yet she did the same thing and locked up behind her.

The snow was falling and her fingers were getting numb. She needed to get back to the library soon. The sun would be going down soon and she didn't want to cross town in the dark with so many undead still roaming.

She decided to do something unique before she left. A search of the auto store produced a broken pencil and a sheet of charred paper in a desk. She wrote down her name and the address of the building across the street from the library and slid the note under the locked door.

*   *   *   *   *

Even at the end of the world there were chores to be done. Darlene, wrapped in layers of warm clothing, shoveled snow off the roof of the library.

Without benefit of the news or the Weather Channel, the blizzard had struck without warning overnight, dumping almost a foot of snow on the ground. It was still snowing, but Darlene needed something to do and wanted to clear her lookout spot off on the roof.

She was glad she did, because there was someone standing across the street watching her. And he was alive.

Figuring the noise she was making tossing snow off the roof had given away her position, she waved.

He waved back and moved across the street toward her.

Darlene knew it was a male because of the way he walked. He stood just under her on the front steps, boots hidden in the snowdrift.

"Hello up there."

Darlene smiled. "Hello down there."

"Wondering if I can borrow a cup of sugar?"

Now she was laughing. "Sorry, I'm all out. Did you try the grocery store on the next corner?"

"Yes, but, unfortunately, the owners were pretty mean. In fact, they tried to bite me."

"Customer service." Darlene smacked her gloved hands together. "I'm Darlene."

"Pierce."

"Seriously? That's not a real name."

He laughed and put his hand on his jacket over his heart. "I swear my parents named me that."

"I'll need to see a driver's license." Despite the playful bantering, she was being cautious and only half-joking. She was also getting very cold up here on the roof.

He reached into his pocket and pulled out his wallet. He made a dramatic show of rifling through it before producing his license and holding it up. 'See?"

"Not from here." Darlene hesitated. She'd been fooled before, like when she was passing through Connecticut and that militia group held her captive.

She was lonely for some companionship, someone who she could have an intelligent conversation with. If she wanted to be brutally honest, she was sick of playing with herself and a real, live cock might be good for her, too. Darlene laughed out loud at the images that flooded her mind.

"Is something funny up there?"

Darlene put the shovel over her shoulder. "Can you climb?"

"Yeah." He shrugged. "Why?"

"Because the only way in is getting over the fence in the parking lot, and then I'll have to unlock the back door. Think you can handle that?"

"Sure."

"Good. Now come back tomorrow and bring some food and water with you."

He threw his hands in the air in mock anger. "What? It's cold outside. By tomorrow it will be colder, with eight feet of snow."

"Then make sure you bring back some hot food."

"Would Buffalo wings suffice, my Lady of the Snowdrifts?"

"Make sure you bring plenty of celery and Ranch dressing," Darlene called down.

* * * * *

Pierce brought stale Pringles sour cream and onion chips, a six-pack of spring water, and a box of white rice. They ate, sharing small talk and keeping away from the Big Conversation, the elephant in the corner that was their situation.

When he suddenly leaned over and kissed her, she responded in kind, and took his hand to her breast. In moments, they were tearing at each other, clothes flying and their bodies responding. Darlene didn't know or care how long it had been for him, but she knew it had been too long since she'd had consensual sex.

Consensual sex? How abut being raped by the redneck militia, Darlene thought and quickly regretted it.

"Is something wrong? Is this too fast?" Pierce asked, pulling away from her and genuinely looking worried.

"It's not you, it's me," Darlene said.

Pierce smiled. "Are you breaking up with me?"

Darlene had to laugh. "That did sound bad. No, I've just gone through some pretty bad shit lately."

"I imagine most people have. If you ever want to talk about it, I'm here. I've got nothing else to do."

"I'll be fine, just a brain-fart." Darlene kissed him softly on the lips. He was a good-looking guy, maintaining his personal hygiene with a shaved face, fingernails trimmed, and the hint of shampoo in his groomed hair. "How about you? Anything bad happen to you lately?"

"Besides people trying to eat me? Nah." Pierce looked around from their vantage point on a couch above the main floor of the library. "You've got a nice place here. Read a lot?"

"Really?"

"No." She laughed.

"Got any good porn?"

"Some erotica titles I found, but they get me too worked up." Darlene liked him. She didn't care about the future or anything else. Like Bob Seger said,' we got tonight, who needs tomorrow?' Or something like that.

"I could read to you," Pierce said and grinned. "Where are they hidden?"

"I'm by myself, why would I hide them?" she said but couldn't stop smiling. "They're hidden next to the makeshift bed."

"Exactly. You always hide your porn. If I was the last man on earth I'd still hide my *Playboys*."

"*Playboy?* I've got erotica in my room, some choice sex writing."

"Nice. Mind if I see for myself?"

"Are you trying to get into my room?" Darlene said and stood, taking his hand.

"I'm actually trying to get in your pants, but we'll start with the room."

* * * * *

Darlene woke with the window breaking and reached for her Desert Eagle.

It was dark and frigid cold. Her knees popped. She felt sluggish, but forced herself to move. Pierce, who'd finally relented and moved into the library fortress two weeks ago, was still sleeping.

Outside the converted bedroom, standing at the top of the stairs, Darlene saw her breath in white plumes but nothing else. *Maybe I was dreaming?*

Despite wearing three layers of clothing, two pairs of heavy socks and a woolen hat, she was freezing. Glancing at one of the large overhead windows, she saw nothing. No stars. She hoped it wasn't snowing again.

Stepping quietly down the stairs, she surveyed the room. They'd recently piled up most of the desks, chairs and miscellaneous furniture against the front doors, blocking off the lobby. In the center of the room now stood two comfortable chairs, two stacks of books to read, and a single desk between them. At the time, they'd joked that it was something to do besides complain about the cold, lack of food, and having sex. Of course, right after, they'd had sex.

Now, she could see something lighter than the shadows glittering to her far right. She panicked and almost pulled the trigger before realizing it was falling snow.

"Shit," she whispered. She went back and woke Pierce. "We have a problem."

"Damn it's cold."

"That's the problem." Darlene led him to the main room and they went down the stairs, eyes roaming the darkness. Pierce had a weapon of his own: a machete which he took great pride in oiling and keeping sharp.

"Snow," he muttered.

"No shit," she said playfully. One of the ceiling windows, which in better times added character to the room, now littered their feet in a million shards. A steady plummet of snowflakes fell through the gaping hole.

"You're shaking," Pierce said and put his arms around her. She was shivering, her breath hanging in front of her face. "Your teeth are chattering. It's really annoying,   that   sound."

"You   know   what's   really   annoying?" Pierce kissed her cold ear and she shuddered, half from the cold and half from his touch. "Tell me."

"That we didn't meet under better conditions."

"What could be better than this? Literally freezing to death, snow threatening to bury us, zombies trying to chew on my man-junk like a toy... oh, and we're starving."

"You have such a way of making me forget our problems." Darlene snuggled close to him. "That was sarcasm,   by   the   way."

"We need to build a fire. Thirty blankets aren't cutting it anymore, especially tonight. We'll be frozen by   morning   with   this   new   problem."

"No fire." Darlene felt her fingers tingling and knew frostbite was a very real threat. "That will only alert the living and the dead where we are."

"The living wouldn't be a problem. Strength in numbers, I say. There might be people a block away from us that need help or can help us get out of here and move south." Pierce rubbed his exposed cheeks. "If we don't light a fire, we'll die. It's as simple as that."

"Fuck." Darlene looked up at the gaping hole in the ceiling again. As if in response to her worries, a large piece of glass crashed down, the fresh pile of snow on the floor cushioning the sound. "Let's pile up some books, but we need to find a spot where the smoke isn't seen for miles and it doesn't choke us to death,   either."

"Not a problem. I'll get some kindling." Pierce smiled. "Would you prefer we start by burning children's books or reference books?"

"Anything with a zombie in it. I've had enough of them for a lifetime."

"I'll see what I can do. I guess we'll need the piles of blankets and clothes down here with us. Do you mind?"

"No." Darlene kissed him lightly on his cold cheek. "We're going to run out of food and drink soon."

Pierce put his head down. "How many days do you think we have?"

"If we eat conservatively we have about two weeks. The problem is the places closest to us have been picked clean."

"I say we leave tomorrow for the south. I hear Florida is nice this time of year," Pierce said.

"I need to get back to Maine."

"I'm thinking if Baltimore has a foot of snow right now, Maine has eight. You'll never make it."

And there it was, Darlene thought. He didn't say 'we'll never make it'. She was a fling, an escape for a few weeks or months, a quick fuck until something better came along. Even at the end of the world, Darlene was being screwed over by some guy she'd just met. *Stupid,* *stupid.*

Pierce turned away and began gathering books.

*   *   *   *   *

Darlene tried to justify her actions: he was using her, the library was too cold with the hole, the fire would eventually draw unwanted attention, she was better on her own, and she saw no future with Pierce. "Future? That's really funny," she whispered.

It had stopped snowing sometime in the early morning hours. With Pierce wrapped up in at least four covers, his back to the smoldering fire and snoring softly, she'd risen and gathered her meager belongings. She pondered taking half the food, roughly twenty cans, but decided against it.

Filling her pockets with three cans of food and one of the can openers, she sneaked outside into the parking lot.

A lone zombie was struggling through a snowdrift across the street but it hadn't seen her. She waited in the still, cold air as the sun tried to break free from the clouds.

"Which way to go?" she whispered.

She could head north towards Maine and hope someone – anyone – she'd known was still alive. She wondered if south was a better move; get out of this cold weather. As much as she'd complained about bad weather reports on the news, having a report was better than looking out the window and figuring it out on her own.

As she stood there freezing, she decided south was the better choice. Darlene advanced through the snow.

*   *   *   *   *

Gray plumes of smoke mixed with the gently falling snow, creating a fog-bank effect. Darlene couldn't see more than ten feet in front of her. Twice, she'd stumbled into a zombie buried in the snow. Her left boot had a gash in it from one biter and her socks and feet were soaked. She prayed frostbite wouldn't be a problem.

When she got closer to the actual fire, she had to laugh. The movie theatre where she'd first met Pierce was ablaze, the diner before it already gutted and smoldering.

She heard snow crunching behind her and turned to see three zombies, all formerly women, moving slowly towards her. One twisted an ankle and went down, disappearing for a brief moment in the snow before her dirty claws reemerged and she tried in vain to pull herself up in the soft snow.

It was easy to sidestep them and go back the way she'd come because the route south was blocked. Darlene was almost as slow as the undead, and that scared her. She would tire in this mess, while they could keep on stumbling along and eventually pounce on her.

Another noise to her left made her realize that while she'd been moving south, a group of zombies had been tailing her. Now they were spread out in the street before her, some caught in the snowdrifts.

"Fuck," she whispered. Leaving like this had been ridiculous and suicidal. For what? Because of an expression Pierce had used? Really? Had he done anything to make her think that he was going to abandon her? Anything at all?

"Stupid bitch," she murmured to herself as she moved as quickly as she could. She'd grown up in Maine and knew how to traverse the snow well enough, but she'd never done it while being chased by zombies who wanted to rape her.

Three long blocks later she had put some distance between her and her attackers but she was winded. She glanced back to see at least twenty of them following slowly and silently, the plodding of so many feet in the snow unnerving.

"Pierce!" she yelled when she got in view of the library. He was on the roof, shoveling. She tried to run and wave at the same time.

He glanced down at her but didn't respond.

"Help! I need the gate opened, I can't climb it."

Pierce didn't say a word, just stood above her with the shovel.

Darlene pointed at the gate.

She could hear them behind her, inching closer.

"Hello?" she waved up at him. "A little help would be nice." *Don't panic, don't fucking panic.*

"I thought you were leaving," he finally said.

"Who said that?"

"I said it. I watched you get dressed, steal food, and slip out." Pierce waved the shovel in front of him. "You'd better keep moving before they fuck you."

"You sonofabitch! Open this fucking gate!"

Pierce stooped and scooped some snow from the roof, depositing it on Darlene below. "Nope."

She felt something cold touch her face and swung around without looking, connecting with a dead face. Darlene staggered to the locked gate and willed her body to respond as she tried to climb.

A zombie grabbed her ankle but she managed to kick it away, getting farther up the chain-link fence. She was halfway to the top and feeling confident that if she could just slip over the top, she'd be free. She'd deal with Pierce later – thinking about her Desert Eagle if she had to use it – but right now, she needed to simply survive.

The sudden pain in her ankle was brutal. Darlene looked down to see a tall, thin male zombie sinking his rancid teeth into her flesh right through her boot.

I'm bit, I'm fucking bit... after all that I've been through, killing my dad, getting raped by those militia jerk-offs, almost dying from a hundred other zombies and the living alike, to have it end here, hanging from a fence...

Darlene pulled the Desert Eagle and fired a single shot into its head, satisfied that it would never bite someone again. Despite the throbbing from the bite, she managed to get the rest of the way over the fence and dropped down into a snow bank. Inches away, at least twenty zombies slammed against the fence, hands and arms reaching for her.

She packed the bite – already red and black and bubbling – with snow.

Her shot had alerted another score of undead to her position.

"Pierce? Open the door."

He actually did open the door a crack on the other side of the parking lot, peeking out. "You were bit."

"It was just a scratch. I'm fine."

"Bullshit."

"I swear. Help me in, I think I busted my ankle."

"You were bit, you lying bitch. I saw it." Pierce started to close the door.

"Wait! Why are you doing this?"

"Go to Hell, zombie."

"Asshole." Darlene crawled behind a car in the parking lot to escape the prying eyes of the undead and so she could have her last meal of cold corn and soup, waiting for the poison to course through her veins and turn her into one of them.

She hoped she had the strength to get the door open and see Pierce one last time.

Chapter Twelve

Frozen Blood

Somehow she'd managed to crawl under the car and fallen asleep. She dreamed of fire, zombies and gunshots.

Her eyes opened slowly, adjusting to the unnatural light. It was nighttime and freezing cold, but the car above her was aflame. Several bodies were alight near her, casting much-welcomed heat. Darlene pulled out her trusted Desert Eagle and scampered from beneath the car, careful to keep from being burned.

Legs stiff from disuse and from the bone-chilling cold, she stood on wobbly legs and searched the parking lot. At least a dozen bodies littered the surrounding area, three cars and several bodies ablaze.

She glanced up to the roof of the library and saw that her makeshift fire buckets had been used, spilling debris, flammables and oil down to the ground, where they'd caught fire.

The fence to the parking lot had been ripped apart as well as the back door to the library. Darlene didn't know which way to go. There were no zombies on the streets but that could change at any moment.

Inside were likely more zombies, either attacking Pierce or already turning him. "Food and blankets are also inside," she whispered. Despite her lying about her ankle being broken, it still hurt where she'd been bit. She needed to wash it soon. She fought back the thoughts of why she wasn't undead yet.

If she left now – and she thought that north was the only way passable to her – she would need supplies.

"Inside it is," she whispered. It had stopped snowing but the sky was a pillow of soft white and she knew it would begin again.

The doorway was a black mouth, a stark contrast to the piles of white surrounding it. Darlene didn't see movement as she approached.

She wondered if Pierce was alive. Even though he'd left her for dead, refusing to open the gate or the door and save her from the zombie horde at her back, she still had to admit that the short time they'd spent together had been good. The sex had been more than good, she mused. Being with another person had been wonderful, able to talk and laugh and help one another. "If I hadn't tried to run out on him, would things be different?" She didn't know.

Her instinct had been Pierce was going to leave her, so she decided to go first instead of waking to find him gone. All that had done was bring back the undead to the library and destroy it, get her bitten and probably infected – although, when was this evil change supposed to take effect? – and get Pierce killed as well. Her plan to head south to safety had blown up in her face. *Monumental failure.*

Swallowing her fear she stepped over the threshold and moved slowly down the hallway. The main room of the library, despite having a gaping hole in the ceiling where the weight of the snow had opened it, was warmer than outside. Not much, but enough to know the difference.

Six bodies, ripped apart by bullets, were tossed across the floor. Darlene looked to the spiraling staircases but didn't see anyone on the landing. None of the bodies were Pierce. He had to be upstairs.

Her ankle wasn't broken but it hurt like Hell as she ascended the steps. There was frozen blood on the steps and pieces of flesh. None of it was Pierce, as far as she knew.

She peeked around the corner as soon as she got to the landing. Three undead stood in front of the door to the room that she'd occupied with Pierce up until she'd left. They weren't slamming against the door, weren't scratching or trying to break it down. Instead, they stared with unseeing eyes.

Her machete still at her side, she decided to use it instead of her pistol in such close quarters. Regardless of whether Pierce was alive or not, she needed to get in there and gather the supplies.

The first zombie took two chops to sever its neck before the others had even turned. Darlene stepped back and was glad the other two collided with one another in their haste to get at her. She swung and connected with an upraised arm.

Taking steps back to the landing, making sure nothing was climbing behind her, she whipped the machete around and it dug into the neck of a zombie. She almost panicked when it stuck, but instead of freaking out she kicked the thing in the stomach and dislodged her weapon.

In no time she'd finished the pair off, kicking them into the corner of the landing as far from the stairs as she could.

She went to the door and listened. Was that Pierce breathing?

"Pierce," she finally asked. She pulled the Desert Eagle.

At first she heard nothing but just as she reared back to kick the door open she heard his thin voice, but couldn't understand what he was saying.

Darlene kicked it open the door, shattering it as it slammed against the wall. The room was just as she'd left it so many hours ago: food and supplies piled in one corner, their bedrolls, pillows and blankets heaped under the shuttered window, and clothes stacked on the far wall.

What was different was the amount of blood that coated everything. At quick glance she noted at least seven bodies in various states around the room, limbs, fingers, and heads everywhere.

Pierce, his stomach a jumbled mess of spilling blood and guts, was leaning against the supplies. His breath came in short, frozen gasps. His eyes lit up when he saw Darlene.

Darlene was impressed with the fight Pierce had put up in this room. "You're hurt," she finally said to him.

"Just a flesh wound," he whispered and laughed, a trace of blood flecking the corner of his mouth. "I need a stiff drink and some bandages. I'll live."

"You've been bit."

"So have you." He glanced at her ankle. "Why are you still able to talk?"

"Just a flesh wound," she said.

Pierce closed his eyes, his chest heaving.

She could see he'd been bit multiple times, the black poison coating his veins and slowly working through his bloodstream. Both legs and arms were gray, his neck a dark smudge of blacks and blues.

"Help me," he whispered. "I need a bandage."

Darlene decided that she needed to head north as soon as possible. She'd gather as much as she could carry, eat whatever food she couldn't, and set the library ablaze. Hopefully it would attract any zombies in the area.

Pierce opened his eyes and stared at her.

"Go to Hell, zombie," she finally said and put a bullet through his head.

Chapter Thirteen

Heading Out To The Highway

The Jaguar XJ didn't miss a beat as Darlene cut the wheel back and forth, avoiding abandoned cars and rubble on I-95. She refrained from putting a CD in and blasting music while she drove.

She glanced up but there were no clouds in the sky, just a perfect clear day. It was still cold but as she continued south the snow had turned to rain and than cleared up.

Her immediate plan was to head north and back home but everything in that direction was aflame, and with snow falling at an alarming rate she decided to move in the opposite direction.

The Jaguar had Maryland plates but she was already crossing into Georgia. Getting gasoline was the toughest part, since she had to siphon from other cars.

The backseat was filled with boxes of miscellaneous food she'd pilfered from a few stores on her journey, and a score of fifty twenty-ounce water bottles.

Darlene hoped there were survivors in Florida, which she figured would be her eventual final destination. "There has to be communities that pushed back the undead and rebuilt, right?" she whispered.

A pileup ahead slowed her down, and she zigzagged in and out of cars, but she kept it moving. That was a good thing, because she cut around a torched van and suddenly there were six zombies on either side of her. Her initial reaction was to take her foot off the gas.

She floored it but did it so suddenly that the back tires spun on the pavement and she didn't move. A zombie reached into the open window and gripped her arm.

The car lurched but Darlene didn't have her hands on the wheel when it took off. She punched ineffectively with her left hand at the zombie, keeping the teeth away from her.

The Jaguar slammed into a tree on the side of the road at around twenty miles an hour, jarring Darlene and tossing the zombie.

"Motherfucker," she screamed, tasting blood in her mouth where she'd bitten her tongue. She exited the car and pulled her Desert Eagle.

The zombie was scrambling to get back on its feet but Darlene put it down for good with a headshot.

With renewed calm she walked back to the pileup and shot each zombie in the head in turn. Satisfied that there were no more in the immediate area, she went in search of a new car and bullets.

* * * * *

The wind blew through her hair as Darlene opened the Chrysler Sebring convertible up on a long stretch of open road, hitting ninety. She decided she'd listen to music and searched for any CD's in the car while she drove. "Something light and happy would be great," she whispered.

PART TWO

DYING DAYS

Chapter One

Lazy Eye held the pistol to Darlene's head and licked his lips. "I said to take your fucking clothes off."

Darlene held her hands up and away from her body. "Is that a two-twenty six?"

Lazy Eye looked confused. He shook the pistol and motioned at her with his free hand. "I won't ask again."

"I think you're right about that." Darlene slipped her head down and to the left, bringing her extended fingers up and into his throat. Before he'd even stumbled she had gripped his arm, dislodged the pistol and heard his shoulder pop out of its socket.

Lazy Eye went to scream but she covered his mouth, drove her knee into his stomach, and picked up the pistol in seconds.

"Shut the fuck up or I will shoot you, motherfucker." She had no intention of actually shooting him, since they were surrounded by undead. None of them were close enough to be an immediate threat, but they were there. The gunshot would get them moving toward her for miles out here.

Under her the man struggled vainly. Darlene pointed the pistol at his head and he finally took the hint and stopped struggling. "This is a Sig Sauer 226 model, and a nice one at that. You don't strike me as being a Navy SEAL or a Texas Ranger, so I'm guessing you found it. Too bad. It's an excellent piece. Mind if I keep it?"

Lazy Eye didn't say anything. His good eye focused on her face before looking down at her dangling boobs at eye level. He licked his lips again.

"Idiot." She sat up, pulled a hunting knife from her boot and shook her head. "Here you go; the last thing you'll ever see." With that she pulled her dirty T-shirt top up and revealed her tits to the man, who openly drooled on the ground.

"Nice, I know." Darlene leaned close to him and just as his fingertip brushed against her hard left nipple she plunged the blade into his stomach and twisted. He gurgled as she drove the blade deeper into him and Darlene closed her eyes and tried to think of happy thoughts. She couldn't and began to cry softly. As much as a scumbag as this guy was, he was still living and didn't deserve to die. "Better you than me," she mumbled. She cursed herself for not hearing him sneak up on her to begin with. So busy scanning the distance for the dead she'd not heard the living until he was on her.

At this point in the game the only people still living were usually those stealthy enough, fast enough or lucky enough to keep from being ripped apart. Lazy Eye had obviously been lucky until today.

She cleaned the blade on his clothes and checked him for supplies, food, anything. He had nothing in his pockets. His boots were too big for him and he wore three pairs of socks despite being out in the Florida heat of summer. "Where did you come from?" she whispered to his lifeless body before doing the horrific task of sawing through his neck with her knife to keep him from reanimating and trying to rape her again.

He looked decently well-fed and he'd bathed in the last few days. His underwear was clean and his shirt still had a slight laundry detergent smell to it, something Darlene hadn't smelled in too long. He had a camp somewhere close, possibly a home where he had a makeshift washer.

She was in the dunes near the beach, with several undead lurking on the road behind her. Any noise would alert them. Darlene scanned the beach itself and watched as two zombies shambled from the surf and moved in different directions. They were everywhere.

Three days ago Darlene had cold-camped on a Georgia beach in a lifeguard chair. She'd woken to five zombies chasing after a child, no more than seven, down the sand. Before she could jump down and help three undead fell from the dunes behind her and gave chase as well. It was all she could do to sit in silence without making a sound as more and more came into view and went north in pursuit of fresh prey.

Now, she decided to journey the way Lazy Eye had appeared and see if she could find his camp. The going was slow, especially since she was trying to be as quiet as possible. A dead man, clothes shredded and covering only his shoulders, stumbled a few feet to her left and she froze. His penis was engorged with blood, rivulets dripping from its bloated head. He was one of the dangerous ones: the undead that still had a functioning sexual organ and would love nothing more than to use it on her, stretch her and rip into her and kill her. She shuddered at the thought.

Five tense minutes later he suddenly stopped and turned away from her and crashed through the sand toward the road. Darlene continued to move as the sun beat down upon her, sun-burnt and hurting. Six or seven months ago she was freezing, stuck in a blizzard during winter near Baltimore. She'd nearly died from sickness and watched as the living around her had succumbed to frostbite or the undead that hadn't frozen. She imagined that by now they'd thawed out and were hunting for the living.

A service road came into view, devoid of immediate danger. She joined the sandy strip up into the dunes. From this vantage point she could see for miles: A1A ran from north to south, riddled with moving bodies; a small town was to the west, smoldering and destroyed; and to the north over a collapsed bridge stood a gas station, which looked intact from this distance. She decided to head for it. Maybe there was some food left over, a stray can of soda. Crumbs would suffice at this point. Darlene hadn't eaten since yesterday morning and that meal was a rotting orange and some rain water. For weeks she'd stayed away from mirrored surfaces when possible, knowing that her once full figure was now a mess. "Even at the end of the fucking world you're still worried about how your ass looks in a tight pair of jeans," she whispered and grinned.

In order to get to the gas station she needed to traverse the broken bridge or wade through fast-moving sea water from the ocean. She didn't know if she had enough strength to make it. That had never stopped her before.

Praying to a God she no longer believed in, she moved slowly in that direction, skirting the undead and glad that they were so spread out.

She wondered why there were so many zombies concentrated in this strip of land. Once she'd gotten safely across the river and onto A1A she thought she'd be safer. With the Atlantic Ocean to the east and the river to her west, land consisted of a block or two of houses in length at any given point, but where she stood there wasn't much of anything but sand dunes. Usually the dead convened around destroyed towns, burnt-out buildings or car pileups.

There were no undead pulling themselves from the river as she stood on its banks. The bridge was unmanageable to cross, with a large chunk of it missing and presumably sitting at the bottom of the river. Darlene wondered how zombies could destroy a bridge like that, but decided that her fellow humans had most likely done the deed.

Most of the property damage she'd encountered since this had begun was man-made, with looting, raping and fires done without the zombies' help. Man had turned on man. Instead of helping one another they'd decided to kill for that last scrap of food. Safety in numbers? Not if it meant having to share a can of soup. It was easier to bash your former friend and neighbor in the head with the can rather then sharing it.

With the sun overhead and the smell of the water before her, Darlene could almost imagine that everything was normal again. Somewhere a bird actually chirped and she could almost sense the fish in the water and the ants and spiders in the grass. She was on vacation with her father, enjoying the Florida beaches and the warmth before heading back to the harsh Maine winter. They would stop later and eat at an amazing local restaurant that sold fresh seafood platters, local beer, and had tiki torches and real palm trees adjacent to the open-air dining room.

She took in a deep breath to get the rich taste of suntan oil, mixed drinks and fried fish into her nostrils. When she choked on the stench of the undead moving silently toward her she sighed. The machete strapped to her back was quietly unsheathed and she said good-bye to her father and her vacation dreams once again.

Chapter Two

He was alone and his skin was sloughing off from so much time in the seawater. His clothes were missing as well as his left arm and his hair. Darlene stepped back and took a swing with the machete, slicing through its neck like butter. She didn't even wait for him to fall before turning and stepping into the cold water of the river.

How many had she dispatched since it began? How many zombies had she destroyed? How many of the living did she have to kill as well? Barry came to mind, but he was only one of a score of men and women she'd had to fight and put down to keep from being killed herself. The first to die by her hands had been her father...

"Enough of this shit," she whispered and began moving into the water, holding her machete and two guns overhead. Luckily this was a small tributary of the actual river so she got chest-deep into it before it leveled out and she could start rising again. Her head bobbed left to right, left to right, prepared for a zombie to grip her ankle or shoot from the water. Instead, she stood on the far bank and looked around at more dunes and the sand-covered road that led to the gas station. This side of the bridge no zombies were shuffling about. She wanted to be as quiet as she could so that they wouldn't be.

As she approached the gas station she held out the Desert Eagle in her right hand and the machete swinging in her left. She was as wary about zombies as the living at this point. Friends were few and far between. Darlene figured that if there was anything of value in the gas station she'd be fighting for it. Just another day in paradise.

A chain-link fence surrounded the property, barbwire strung across the top. There was no discernable gate as far as she could see. She hated being so exposed but no trees, bushes or even dunes were between the water and the fence.

Darlene hesitated before moving to her left and away from the road leading to the gas station. Behind the property the back road wound up over another, smaller bridge, leading to a two-story house. It, too, was boxed in with the fence. The road leading between the two buildings was fenced in as well. Whoever was up in the house was probably watching her. Even now they would be getting into position with a rifle if they had one, her head in the cross-hairs. She closed her eyes and counted to five.

"I guess not," she whispered when her head didn't explode. It was almost... disappointing that she was still alive. She buried the thought in her head, swimming from the heat, lack of food and water, and the constant fear with each step she took.

To keep her mind off of it she checked and rechecked her weapons and she walked directly to the fence and stared at the gas station. If the owners were going to kill her they didn't have long-range weapons. She guessed that they'd make their way down the fenced-in road soon enough. Best see what the lay of the land was like until the confrontation.

The pumps were still intact, although sand and debris had been flung up and around them. The road itself was nearly obliterated with the natural elements as well. When Darlene noticed that the windows were unbroken and the main door complete she smiled.

Hopping the fence was no easy task in her physical state but she managed it. Her jeans had become snagged on the barbed wire and one leg was shredded. Darlene had to stop at the top and keep her head from swimming and dumping her face-first to the ground. She'd lost way too much way too fast and her muscle mass was being depleted at an alarming rate, but the alternative was much worse. She breathed in the salt air as she approached the gas station with her Desert Eagle drawn.

She hoped that the owners weren't inside.

The windows and doors had been covered from inside with cardboard. *So far, so good.*

The front door was locked as she suspected. She walked slowly around the building, trying to catch a glimpse of anything inside but there wasn't even a crack.

The bay doors to the garage area were chained and padlocked from outside, the large windows covered as well. When Darlene got to the back she glanced at the house but didn't notice any movement. For the moment there was no pursuit and no gunshots.

The back door leading into the garage was unlocked and she hesitated before turning the knob all the way and opening it. Caution made her stare intently at the door frame for tell-tale wiring or booby-traps. She didn't see anything out of the ordinary.

Six nights ago she'd come upon a camp of the living, nestled between a smoldering bowling alley and a dilapidated fast food restaurant. They had somehow dragged a damaged car into the gaps at either end and positioned guards with rifles to watch. She was pondering whether or not to reveal herself and perhaps join them when she tripped over a wire. Luckily it wasn't attached to explosives but simply to rusted cans. When it clanged the alarm, three shots had rung out in quick succession in the general area that she was moments before.

The undead in the area began moving toward them. Darlene had beat a hasty retreat, dodging the undead until she could escape into a used car lot and hide in the flatbed of a Toyota Tacoma until she fell asleep. The next morning there was nothing left of the group except for blood and a few scraps of food.

"Fuck it," she whispered and turned the knob. It didn't explode, no shrapnel flew from a hidden gun, and no green glop fell from the top of the door. Silence greeted her as she stepped inside and shut the door behind her.

It was dark and she waited for her eyes to adjust to the gloom. She held her machete out just in case something dead was moving on her in the blackness.

The garage area was empty save for some grease stains on the cement floor. She hoped that a red tool setup was present so she could find a few weapons: big wrenches, hammers or even a saw. Her machete was getting dull from so much use. She'd need to sharpen it or find another weapon sooner than later.

Even though she could now see that the room was empty, she took her time and stalked around. Maybe something was hidden in a dark corner.

The only thing she found was the door leading into the rest of the gas station. It was also covered with cardboard, which she found odd. Covering the windows leading to the outside made sense.

This door was also unlocked. Again, she checked it for wires before turning the handle completely. Darlene noticed her hand was shaking. Her nerves were shot and she wondered for the hundredth times today whether all of this was worth it or not. She was physically and mentally exhausted, each day another trial and tribulation.

Darlene composed herself and shrugged her aching shoulders. "Get over it, bitch. Time to kill something."

The knob turned easily enough and she swung the door open, leading with the Desert Eagle. The first thing she noticed was the hum of the coffee makers, then the lights glowing from the soda coolers, and then the two men sitting at a table playing cards.

"Deal me in, boys," she said and realized how stupid and cliché it was. Darlene didn't care. The coffee smelled like heaven and she hoped they had cream and sugar.

Chapter Three

"Holy shit," was all one of the men could say before Darlene was upon them, holding the gun to his head.

They were both middle-aged but clean. They smelled of deodorant instead of shit. They wore coveralls and baseball caps, clean sneakers and they were clean-shaven. Darlene hadn't shaved in God-knows how long. *I could scare them with my damn bush*, she thought.

They stood in this pose for at least two minutes, Darlene with the gun to one's head and eyeing both. She had no idea what she was going to do at this point. She was too tired to take them both on and knew as soon as she pulled the trigger on the first one the second was close enough to grab her.

"Can I help you?" the second one managed, hands in the air.

"You can start by getting me a cup of that coffee."

He smiled slightly. "When was the last time you ate?"

"None of your fucking business. Move before your lover here gets his brains splattered on the floor."

"Yes, ma'am. Just relax, we can work this out." The man took three strides to the coffee pots. Darlene pressed the gun to the other's head and tried not to let him see her hand shaking.

"Never tell a woman to relax."

"Sorry," he said as he turned. He had a small-caliber pistol in his hand.

Darlene pulled the trigger on instinct and it saved her life. The explosion of his partner's head wasn't expected and his shot went wide. Darlene shot him in the stomach and he fell to the floor.

When she heard him moaning she swung around the table and leveled the gun at his head. "Move and you die."

"Too late, I think. You bitch." He tried vainly to cover the blood pouring from his midsection. His eyes were already glossing over.

She went to him, standing over him with the gun. "I can end this now or leave you here to bleed to death."

"Doesn't much matter," he choked out the words.

"Oh, but it does." Darlene leaned closer. "All I wanted was some fucking coffee."

He actually laughed at that, and began coughing and screaming in pain.

"Shut up."

He complied.

"It's your choice."

"Kill me," he managed.

"Who's at the house?"

"No one."

"Liar."

"I swear. Joe and I were the last two left. The others turned about a week ago."

"Then why were you sitting here playing cards?"

He coughed blood. She repeated the question.

"Why the fuck not? We had enough food and drink here, and the house was overrun with dead fuckers. We trapped them inside and came out here. What else could we do?"

"It doesn't look like there's a ton of food left in here."

He tried to roll onto his side but she threatened him with a kick and he stopped moving. "The bulk of the food is stacked in the house. There's enough food and water there to last a lifetime. Fucking Gary fucked up. Why did he have to go out and explore? Fuck."

"How many in the house?"

"Eight."

"What about that fucker I met before?"

"Who?"

"The asshole with the lazy eye."

He shook his head. "No idea who you're talking about. We've been cut off from everything since this shit started. We were smart enough to raid two Publix in the area for supplies."

"How is the power on?"

"Shit, the whole grid never shut off. You got power from here to St. Augustine. Fuck," he said and squirmed on the floor. "Shoot me."

Darlene pulled the trigger without preamble and shot him in the head. She hoped the fences around the building would keep the undead out. She was sure they had heard the commotion and gunfire.

At this moment she didn't care. All she wanted was a sip of the coffee. She poured a cup, added powdered creamer and chipped off a chunk of hardened sugar from a bowl, and held the cup to her nose. She remembered this smell, although she knew the coffee was stale, it had been burnt, and watered down. As soon as her tongue touched the hot brew it sent a ripple through her body. She remembered having a favorite coffee mug, a taupe one with an old, grumpy woman on the side. Below her it said '…not before my first sip…' Darlene started to weep softly as she took a seat and held the cup with both hands.

Chapter Four

The undead had heard the gunshots. They came in twos and threes, walking across the channel and standing at the fence, dripping water and body parts. Darlene counted at least twenty at one point, all directly in front of the gas station and bumping against the fence as they tried to move forward. She kept quiet and watched them through a small hole in the cardboard covering the door. After an hour most of them moved off in random directions.

Darlene chewed on her fifth and final beef jerky strip. The two men had minimal supplies. They could have survived about a week on the snacks. Four cans of soup and three vacuum-sealed packs of noodles. Darlene admired what they'd done: the coolers had been cleaned out, and the spoiled milk and flat carbonated beverages replaced by various sizes of containers of water, crammed onto the sliding shelves and stacked inside the coolers themselves. She estimated about three hundred bottles of water, enough to get her through the next six months or so. Not to mention that the faucets in the bathroom still spat water and she could easily refill as she drank.

The candy was all spoiled or stale, and she had enough cigarettes and tobacco products to get lung cancer. Despite what she'd heard, the Twinkies were actually hard. With the air conditioning still working nothing smelled, but there were only a few items that were still edible. The beer had been either finished off or raided a long time ago.

Darlene found some pink women's razors and shaving cream and ventured into the bathroom to shave and wash up. There was plenty of soap and deodorant stacked neatly under the sink, as well as washcloths and ibuprofen bottles. Before attacking the jungle that was her legs and privates she popped three pills and swallowed them with tap water. They scratched down her dry throat.

Her clothes were peeled off and dispatched to the far corner. She wouldn't have been surprised if they had suddenly stood and made a run for it. Right now she'd give anything for a bra that fit and undies that didn't have rips in them.

As she applied shaving cream she couldn't remember the last time she'd been in air conditioning. "You never get used to the smell of the dead or the smell of your own filth," she whispered. Soon the floor was stained with shaving cream, hair and dirt.

On a whim she checked the store for makeup but found none. She went back into the bathroom and finished, scrubbing her face with most of a bar of soap. For the first time in too long she stared at herself in the dirty mirror and cringed. Her cheekbones were sunken, her eyes puffy and red. Her once-lustrous hair hung in knots, her lips chapped and her chin bruised.

Darlene had never been a skinny woman – she preferred thinking of herself as curvy – but now she was downright anorexic. She guessed that she was hovering at around one hundred and five pounds, a far cry from the healthy one-fifty she normally carried. Her body was sore, black and blue covering her legs and arms, and she could spend a week counting all of the cuts across her body.

She stopped looking at herself in the mirror while she gathered her clothes and began the task of washing them under the hot water from the tap. The dirt and grime filled the sink and she noticed for the first time all of the holes and rips in her jeans and T-shirt. She'd need to find new clothing before she had to make her way naked in this dead world.

Sometimes you forget about the things you no longer have, she thought as she eyed a stack of toilet paper rolls. She was going to enjoy her time here, at least until the food ran out. Then it was back into the wild and fending for the next meal.

Later, after a dinner of cold chicken noodle soup and three bottles of water, she took both bodies outside. She didn't have the strength to bury them but figured that tomorrow she would have to. They yielded little in the way of supplies: the keys to the store, house keys she assumed were from the house up the road, a pack of gum, two pocketknives, and a dead cell phone. The small-caliber gun was empty; he'd used his last shot. She left the gun on the ground where he'd dropped it.

Darlene tossed the cell phone around in her hand and laughed. It was funny what people still clung to, even when they were of no practical use. She reached into her pocket and fingered her keychain. Her house key, her car key and the key to her dad's house were there, all useless. Yet she had them with her at all times.

She peeked outside again but there was nothing hanging around the fence. She knew they were out there. They were always out there. The glow from the coolers was enough light to see by, so she didn't have to stumble around in the dark.

Behind the counter were two pillows and three blankets, which Darlene hadn't used in months. Darlene curled up on the floor, wrapping herself in one of the blankets and stuffing both pillows under her head. It wasn't the greatest of comforts but it beat sleeping in trees, under porches and in cold abandoned buildings. Her body, newly cleaned after weeks of dipping into dirty rain water or rivers and oceans, felt relaxed. Her mind was racing and she hoped that she could sleep. *How ironic would that be, if I finally get a decent spot to sleep on, and I can't?*

She woke with a start and fought back an imaginary attacker. It was just one of the blankets that had wrapped around her legs. Her Desert Eagle, never far from her grasp, was put down on the ground next to her. While the floor had been better than being outside, her back hurt and she had a pounding headache.

By playing with the coffee machines she figured out a safe way to make two packs of the noodles and a pot of coffee for breakfast. After eating she cleaned up the store, getting everything of value together on the counter and separating the items into plastic shopping bags. In the cooler she found four cardboard boxes that could hold two dozen bottles of water each, but she had no idea how to then transport them.

Three hours later she had run out of work to do and knew that she had been stalling. She didn't want to go outside and dig two graves for the men. A part of her didn't even care about doing it, but she felt compelled. They had been alive, after all, and it would be proper to bury them and say something.

Back outside the sun was fierce, with no clouds in the Florida sky. The two bodies were right where she'd left them. She wasn't surprised, but then again not much could surprise her at this point. If they had been dancing or missing when she'd come outside it wouldn't have shocked her. In fact, it now disappointed her that she'd have to bury them. She needed a shovel, which she didn't have.

The house up the road was quiet. She wondered if they had a shed out back, and if she could keep enough distance from the house in the event that the undead inside could escape. There were no zombies outside the fence in the immediate area. Darlene decided to chance it. The sandy road leading to the house offered nothing save a few old footprints.

By the time she reached the bridge she was drenched in sweat. "I need another bath," she whispered. From here the grounds were overgrown with weeds poking through the sand. The dirt road was dusty and rutted from long-ago traffic. The front yard had, at one time, been landscaped. A section of stone wall ran the length of the driveway to the left, now showing wear in a spot and leaning back. A line of short bushes had been planted on the right, now all stunted and dead.

The house loomed before her in the midday heat like a creature ready to pounce. The windows had been boarded hastily from outside, the front door jammed with two rocking chairs and nailed shut.

Darlene was holding her breath as she put a hesitant foot on the first step. "Go around to the back," she whispered. She didn't need to be going onto the porch; she already knew what awaited her inside. She felt like the stupid chick in every horror movie that ignores the scary noises downstairs and goes into the basement, clad in her underwear, and then is amazed when an axe is sticking out of her head.

She put her full weight down on her foot. Not a sound. The wooden steps were solid. Gingerly she made it up the remaining four steps and stood at the front door with her Desert Eagle in hand. She didn't have eight bullets left – three in the Desert Eagle, three in the Sig Sauer 226 - or even know if he had been telling the truth about the number inside. Maybe it was one and he wanted to scare her away. Maybe there weren't any dead inside and the house was filled with food and drink, piles of clothing and form-fitting bras and panties with the tags still attached.

The next step forward and the boards creaked.

Darlene fell back when the banging inside started, right in front of her. It sounded like a hundred undead were inside, slamming against the wall. The windows and door shook with the impact.

Scared and ashamed at how easily she'd been rattled, Darlene ran from the porch and around to the back, in search of a shed and a shovel.

Chapter Five

As she finished burying the two men night was falling. The sounds of the trapped had brought more undead to investigate. Darlene counted almost thirty of them on the other side of the fence groaning and reaching for her. She ignored them as best she could.

At first she was going to simply walk up to them and begin smacking them with the shovel, but she knew it would be futile. The fence would keep her from doing permanent damage. In a strange way she was enjoying the company after being alone for so long. Even if her company wanted to rip off her head and fuck her headless corpse.

Back inside she drank more water and made a can of sirloin burger soup. As a kid she'd hated eating soup, but her father insisted on making it a meal at least once per week. She remembered dreading it when her parents came home from food shopping and her father stacked another three cans on the topmost shelf for later in the week.

Exhausted, Darlene checked the locks on the doors, stared into the darkness outside for lights, listened for noises, and then finally turned in for the night.

The next morning she rose, cleaned up, ate more noodle soup, and was mildly disappointed to see that the undead had moved on during the night. She wished she had binoculars so that she could climb onto the roof and see for miles.

With nothing else to do today, she decided to clean. The undead already knew she was here so she decided to see if the radio worked. Maybe they had a CD she could play while she was cleaning. Darlene decided against it, though. The zombies weren't the only thing she had to fear; out here there was probably more than one Lazy Eye and a noise that loud would give her away.

The air conditioning felt nice. She found some over-priced toothbrushes on a shelf peg and decided to give this place a thorough cleaning. A bottle of cheap bleach and some spray bottles of cleaning supplies were in the small stockroom. The mop and mop bucket were both broken and looked like they hadn't been used a long time before the end of the world. It was just as well. For the first time in months Darlene had a task besides finding food, shelter, and trying not to get killed. She dropped to her hands and knees in front of the counter and began to wash the floor, one inch at a time.

The blankets and pillows smelled funky, so they were hand-washed in the sink before she took them outside and draped them over the gas pumps to dry in the ocean breeze.

A lone zombie crested the dunes over the broken bridge, moving away from her. She wondered if they ever stopped, ever grew tired or ever had a real destination in mind when noises didn't compel them to move in a certain direction. Once again she longed for days that were long gone. In movies she used to watch with her father when she was a kid the zombies would come at night, dark and dreary, gray and overcast, with rain and lightning strikes silhouetting the background.

Darlene's reality was even more disturbing: blue, clear skies, the smell of the beach, the sound of the pounding surf, and the undead. She couldn't remember the last time it had rained since she'd been this far south. She wasn't complaining after the long, cold winter in Baltimore, but still… a little rainfall would be nice, something to break up the sun and the heat.

Once again, before going back inside to continue her cleaning project, she stepped around the side of the station and looked at the house.

It was quiet, as she knew it would be. She almost wished they'd found a way out, one at a time, so she could finish them off and grab the treasure inside. She felt like Laura Croft or Indiana Jones, only they weren't too scared to kick down the door and start shooting and killing with a trusted machete. Instead, she decided to go inside and keep scrubbing with a damn toothbrush.

At first the noise was so unexpected and so far away that she ignored it and went back inside. It seemed like a distant memory. Every now and then, especially after a fitful night of nightmares, she would sometimes wake and hear a voice or a radio playing or traffic in the distance. Fully awake she would cease to hear anything but the wind or the undead.

As it got closer she stopped and stared at the ceiling. "What the Hell?" she whispered. Back outside she stared at the sky.

She heard a plane.

"Where are you?" Darlene spun in a circle, looking and looking. There was no cloud cover. It grew louder, the sound of the engine. It might be a Cessna, something small. It wasn't a commercial airliner. *Did it matter at this point, anyway?*

Darlene couldn't remember the last time a plane, helicopter or air balloon had been spotted in the sky. She shielded her eyes from the glare and wished there was a sunglass rack inside. It made her laugh to think of her standing out here with a pair of huge white tourist sunglasses on and one of those huge weaved hats on her head.

She was positively giggling by the time the plane, indeed a Cessna, shot overhead from the west, glided straight out to sea and then shot up the coast to the north.

Immediately a score of zombies appeared and began to follow the smoke trail in the sky.

Darlene ran inside, locked up, grabbed two bags of groceries, and decided to follow.

Chapter Six

She lost sight and sound of the plane by the time she hopped the fence. Getting back across the water was easier because it was low tide, but she still watched for submerged undead. Back across she moved as fast as she could on A1A. A mob of zombies were ahead of her, following the plane. She knew from experience that they would give up once it was completely gone. She didn't want to be around when that happened. A single zombie or even two or three wasn't a problem in wide open spaces, but twenty or thirty could easily surround you or trip you up.

After half a mile the undead began veering off into random directions. Most of them moved toward the east and the beach. Three stayed course on the road. Trying to be as quiet as possible while still moving, Darlene quickened her pace and was soon past them. One of them grunted but when she saw that none were before her she began to jog.

Bad move.

The noise of her bags jangling brought two undead from out of nowhere, directly in her path. She shouldered through them, getting slashed with rotting fingernails as she moved. Now she was running. Two abandoned cars were in the road and she stayed as far away as possible. It was a good thing because a zombie, legless, was behind the lead car. She could hear its jaws snap as she ran past.

Up ahead, about a quarter mile, a solitary zombie was heading north. Darlene slowed her pace and watched it. She was breathing heavily from her short run and was frustrated to be so out of shape. "You're fucking thirty-five, not eighty-five," she whispered.

The zombie suddenly fell forward and was gone.

Darlene stopped and looked around. Only open road and sand greeted her. She walked quickly to the spot where the zombie had been and saw a crater in the road. Ten feet below the zombie struggled to move, run through on a bevy of sharp wooden spikes in the hole. He wasn't alone. Three more had been caught as well, their bodies falling to pieces on the spikes. Darlene looked around again. The trap was man-made, running across the road. To either side large wooden stakes had been driven into the dunes at angles meant to impale.

On the other side of the pit she noticed several tripwires. The dunes to the west were covered in short pieces of sharpened metal. She'd have to proceed with caution. The paranoid feeling of being watched came over her and she ducked down instinctively and moved toward the beach, careful to watch what she was stepping on.

The waves were strong today, slapping against a horrific sight: a whale, half submerged in the surf, was being eviscerated by a group of zombies. Darlene nearly puked when she saw one of them trying to ejaculate on the dead, bloated creature as other zombies pulled off chunks of flesh. The scene was surreal; gulls fought with the zombies for pieces. She wasn't surprised when one of the gulls got too close and his head was promptly bitten off.

Sticking to the dunes, Darlene tried to ignore the scene and not fall apart. She'd seen some disgusting things in the last few months, things that might have made the old her go mad. Now she tried to chalk it up to just another nauseating sight in the long line of many. There were plenty more in her future, she guessed.

She supposed that the secret was to keep moving and not think too long on any one thing. When this first started she tried to think of pleasant thoughts like vacations on the Maine coast as a child or going to see the Red Sox with her family or playing in the park at the end of her street. Nightmares about zombies coming out of the surf, Fenway Park overrun by the undead and other children dismembered on the slide and the swings at the park forced her to look ahead. *Always look ahead.*

She circumvented the road pit about two hundred feet north before trying to get on stable ground once again. The road was devoid of footprints and traps. Up ahead a charred school bus was on its side, blocking the path. To either side the sand had built up, creating an effective barrier. Darlene doubted that it was natural.

There was no movement from inside or around the bus but she proceeded with caution. If there was going to be an ambush – from undead or living – this would be perfect. She had the machete and the Desert Eagle at the ready as she took tentative steps forward, eyes darting all around her.

To the right, closest to the beach, was a path through the dune. She could either try to climb the bus or follow the trail and go around it via the beach.

Ignoring a nagging feeling in her head, Darlene moved quickly, leading with the machete. The dune sloped up and it was a hard climb. When she reached the top, she slid down, then ran onto the beach and stopped. A crude wooden fence had been built on the sand to the north, braced with debris and car parts, creating an effective barrier for the thirty or forty zombies that were trying to move past it.

"What the Hell?" Darlene managed before the group turned as one and began moving toward her. She knew that climbing the loose sand behind her would only get her caught so she decided to make her stand. If today was the day to die, so be it.

Instead of standing back and letting them come to her she took the battle to them, slicing at the closest with the machete and connecting with its arm. The limb was tossed through the air. Moving to her left, she chopped at another. Her goal was to get to the fence and try to climb over before she was grabbed and killed.

A zombie to her right suddenly staggered, its head shattered. A thick arrow protruded from it. She caught a glimpse before it fell and was swallowed up by the moving horde.

She glanced to the north, in the direction she assumed the arrow had come from, just as another was shot from above on the dune. It ripped into the face of a zombie. Darlene thanked whoever was helping her out and slashed and jabbed with the machete, dropping two more as she got closer to the fence.

She was a whirlwind of motion, clearing a path before her. Arrows filled the air around her. A zombie stood between her and the fence. As she swung to decapitate it she felt a stinging in her left arm.

Looking down, she saw the blood and the arrow, which had neatly pierced her forearm and lodged the tip into her side. She made a frantic swing of the machete at the nearest undead but her vision clouded.

She fell to one knee, still trying to defend herself, as the darkness overtook her.

Chapter Seven

Darkness.

Not gloomy like the middle of the night, sleeping under a cloudy sky with the undead all around you. This was black, stifling, closing in on her. Darlene tried to scream but her throat was too tight, her body unable to move. The night had weight and it was pressing against her, holding her under like an ocean.

"Fuck," she managed to croak and turn on her side. There was a bed under her, soft covers and pillows. The air was cool, and she heard the distant hum of a central air unit. She smelled bacon cooking. She stretched her legs and thought she was dreaming.

A pain shot up her side and her left arm and she nearly passed out. She was awake, unfortunately. She remembered the fight on the beach and the arrow. Gingerly she felt her arm. It was bandaged, as well as her side. She realized with a start as she came fully awake that she was naked.

She rose on wobbling legs, her feet touching cold tile floor. Reaching in the dark, she found an end table and a lamp with her fingers. She clicked the button, figuring that it was futile. Instead, the lamp came to life, casting the room in a soft glow.

The bedroom was small. The bed, covered in navy blue sheets and six matching pillows, was only part of the meager furnishings. The end table with lamp and a plush chair in the corner were the other half. She moved slowly, her body stiff and her arm and side on fire, to the door she figured was the closet. It was empty.

She opened the other door to a dark hallway. Beyond it a candle was lit on a kitchen table and she smelled bacon again. Her mouth watered.

"Are you awake?" a male voice asked softly from the kitchen.

Darlene was startled. It sounded like her father. But her father was... unconsciously she went for her Desert Eagle but it was gone. "Where are my clothes?"

"Oops. Sorry. They just came out of the dryer."

"Dryer? Where the fuck am I?"

The man laughed, his silhouette suddenly blocking the candle. He was big, wearing dark clothes and some sort of hat. He was covering his face with one arm and holding a laundry basket with the other. "Sorry, I lost track of time. Here are your clothes. I took the liberty of washing them, although they are a bit rough. You'll find some undergarments in there that might fit you, they are brand new. Some shirts and a pair of jeans John-John thought might fit you."

When Darlene didn't move the man placed the basket slowly on the floor and walked back into the kitchen.

"Where are my weapons?" she asked, scampering to the clothes and grabbing them. She stepped back into the room, keeping the hall and kitchen in her sights.

"I cleaned the Desert Eagle. Nice piece. The Sig Sauer is actually mine. Your machete is pretty rusted and nicked, but I imagine I could sharpen it for you."

Darlene dumped the clothes on the bed. Her ripped undies were there but a new pair of black thongs was a better choice. She slipped them on. They were a tad small but they hugged her skinny hips and didn't dig too deep into her ass crack. A black T-shirt and tight blue jeans were perfect. She almost cried when she saw white socks, actual white and not gray, and smelling of liquid Tide and not puddle water. Her sneakers had been cleaned a bit, although they had multiple holes in them.

"Where am I?" she asked.

There was a pause as dishes were clanged. "I won't bite you. You're a guest in my home. Please join me for breakfast."

Darlene went down the hall and stepped into the kitchen. It was small and cozy, with wood paneling covering the walls. The small window over the sink had been covered with a painting – Darlene recognized it as a reprint of Van Gogh's *Starry Night*. Her mother had the same print above the television in her living room. The kitchen table was covered with boxes of ammunition, tools and electronic instruments.

Despite the candles spaced on the counters, Darlene could see that the electricity was working. The refrigerator hummed and she could hear the ice maker working. The bags she'd taken with her were sitting on the far counter.

Bacon was sizzling in a frying pan on the stove, a plate of scrambled eggs nearby. "Want toast with that? I have strawberry jam."

"Sure." Darlene was motioned to take a chair at the table. While she pushed boxes of shotgun shells to one side she stared at the man.

He was in his mid-sixties, with a shock of gray hair under a John Deere baseball cap. His clean-shaven face wore a mischievous smile. He winked at her with clear and piercing blue eyes. He whistled off-key as he sliced from a loaf of bread. "Just be a second," he said over his shoulder. "Have a good sleep?"

"I guess." Darlene remembered her manners. "Do you need any help?"

"Nah. Almost finished." He put two pieces of bread into the toaster on the near counter. "Actually, you can fetch us a couple of cold beers from the fridge."

"Isn't it morning?"

He shrugged and laughed, almost choking as he tried to stop himself. "It's actually about noon, little lady, and high time for a beer. When's the last time you had a cold one?"

"I can't remember." Darlene stood and went to the fridge, feeling safe but off-kilter in the home and with this stranger. "I'm Darlene, by the way. Darlene Bobich."

'You can call me Murph." He slid the bacon off of the skillet and onto a paper towel on a plate. "Give me a Bud, if you don't mind."

The refrigerator was loaded with items Darlene thought she'd never see again: four different kinds of beer, a plastic jug of milk, a small tub of butter, bags of various vegetables, and bottles of ketchup and mayonnaise.

"How is it possible you have all of these... luxuries?" she asked.

"We trade with a nearby city. They have animals and we're able to get a few farm fresh items."

She pulled a Bud and a Corona and sat back down. Her plate was waiting and she nearly drooled at the sight.

"Toast will be right up. Did you say yes to jam?"

"Yes, yes." Darlene wanted to wait for her host but Murph must have seen her staring at the food.

"Eat, Jesus, girl, don't wait for me. I'll catch up." The toast popped and he tossed it onto a plate. "I have too much food here sometimes." He turned to her and winked. "You happen to be visiting at one of those times."

The eggs tasted like heaven, the bacon like sex. She ran her fingers around the plate when she thought he wasn't looking, getting every last crumb into her mouth.

Murph laughed when he sat down across from her and handed her a slice of jam-covered toast. "I guess you were hungry, Darlene Bobich. Can't say I'm surprised. You seem absolutely wasting away to nothing. Those clothes were hanging off of you."

She gripped the toast but hesitated to bite it. "Who undressed me?"

Murph's face grew red and he put his head down. "I did. I needed to dress that nasty wound, and your clothes were falling off."

"Thank you," she whispered.

"You're welcome." He looked up at her. "I didn't do anything to you, just so you know. I'm a gentleman, by and by."

Darlene smiled and bit into her divine toast. "I'm afraid my best years are behind me."

Murph laughed. "I may be sixty-six but I'm still a man. You clean up nicely. There's a shower down the hall when you're done with breakfast."

"Thought this was lunch."

"In today's world, I can call this Murph-meal and no one could argue, right? The rules have all changed."

"I suppose you're right."

"I think your arm will be just fine. The arrow poked right through without hitting anything vital. It only skinned your side. It might be sore for a few weeks but you'll live."

"Thanks. Who shot me? You?"

"Nah, I'm not that good a shot anymore. Twenty or thirty years ago I would have killed you, and you'd have been dead before the arrow was through your skull."

"Pleasant."

"Um, sorry." Murph scooped up some scrambled egg. "John-John shot you."

"Who's that?"

"My son. He'll be around shortly. He came by to see you yesterday but you were still sleeping."

"How long have I been here?"

"Almost three days. You had a fever and lost a lot of blood." Murph put down his fork. "You also gave me a scare with that nasty bite on your ankle. It seemed to be... old."

Darlene stood suddenly and grabbed her plate. "I'll do the dishes if you want. That would be fair."

"Don't worry about that. Go take a shower; there are some towels and pajamas that should fit you in there already."

"Thank you for everything."

"Don't mention it."

Darlene tried to ignore Murph when he glanced at her ankle as she went past him and went to take a real shower.

Chapter Eight

"Care for a pinch?" Murph asked Darlene, holding out some tobacco from a plastic bag.

"Not a fan, but I'm glad for the beer." Darlene leaned back on the couch and put the cold Corona to her forehead. She was sweating despite the air conditioning. "All I'm missing is a lime."

"I could probably get a few." Murph put the pinch in his mouth and grinned. "I went almost a year without. I'd rather die than be without it. Everyone needs a vice, right?"

"I guess so." Darlene closed her eyes. After the shower she felt tired again, but at least she finally had real shampoo and hot water in her hair. Murph had even put some mascara and lip gloss in the bathroom, which she took her time applying.

"You look better, especially with the makeup."

Darlene must have given him a look because he put his hands up. "I'm just saying that you clean up better, that's all. Shit, I'm too old for you, missy. I have a daughter your age." Murph looked away. "Had a daughter."

Darlene sat up. "Want to talk about it?"

"Shit, what's to talk about? Ninety percent of the world died and tried to kill the other ten percent. We happen to be the unlucky ten percent. I'm sure everyone and everything you loved is long gone as well. No use crying over it."

"I guess so. Want a beer?"

"Nah, but feel free to drink me out of house and home."

Darlene laughed. "I'd be more than happy to help around this place. It could use a woman's touch."

"I suppose so. I can always get more beer."

"How?"

"That's a trade secret, missy."

Darlene went to the refrigerator and grabbed the last Corona. "Where in Hell are we, anyway?"

"We're about five miles from Hammond Beach, and about twenty south of St. Augustine."

"How are we safe?"

Murph laughed and slapped his knee. "I forgot. You were passed out when John-John brought you here. Come with me."

He led her through the front door. A cool ocean breeze made her smile as she stepped out onto a porch and stared at the ocean. The sun was setting behind her, shadows under the house. "We're in a stilt house?" she said with a laugh.

"Twenty feet above the ground. They can't reach us up here. Or there," Murph said and pointed to a nearby house. "Or there." Darlene counted ten stilt houses strung across the beach in a perfect line. "Every house is occupied or was occupied."

"By who?"

"Survivors. Let's get inside before we're spotted."

"By who?"

Murph laughed. "The living bastards that can still climb a ladder."

Back inside, they took their spots in the living room. Murph sat down in a well-worn chair and put his feet up on the coffee table. "I'd still give my left one for a nice Big Mac."

"I never thought I'd have a breakfast of bacon and eggs again."

"I have some fish in the freezer for tomorrow. Most nights I make some grilled veggies and toss in a baked potato. Sound good?"

"If you let me I can make something special."

"I'm listening."

Darlene rose and went to the kitchen. "I can make a stew with the potatoes and veggies. Do you have cans of chicken broth?"

"I think I have two cans of beef broth in the cabinet. Never knew what to do with them."

"Perfect. Come on, Murph, I'm going to teach you how to make Bobich Stew."

"Sounds like a plan."

Together they cooked, Murph following directions and cutting the vegetables while Darlene prepared the potatoes and the broth. Once dinner was ready they went back to their spots and ate in silence.

"I'll clean the dishes. Least I can do." Darlene was feeling a bit tipsy from the beer and after the great meal she wanted to crawl back into that bed and sleep for a week.

"I need to dress that wound again," Murph said. "Don't want my new houseguest up and dying on me. Especially since she can cook and do dishes."

Darlene tensed when she heard footsteps outside. She went for her Desert Eagle, still on the table, but Murph waved her off. "It's John-John. He does that tapping noise on the top of the ladder to let me know it's him."

"You can't be too safe."

"I agree."

The door opened and John-John stepped inside, carrying a backpack and a compound bow over his shoulder. His blue eyes locked onto Darlene. When she smiled at him he looked away and put his gear down.

"What kind of bow is that?" she asked.

"Jennings Cobra. I have three of them."

"Nice. What kind of arrows do you use?"

John-John shrugged. "Whatever I can find. We raided a sporting goods store about six months back and found a pallet of them, all different kinds."

"He's gotten pretty good at it. He can hit a zombie in the face from a hundred feet," Murph said.

"I guess I got lucky you hit me here," Darlene said and gently tapped her arm.

John-John gritted his teeth. "You had no business trying to fight so many of them. I couldn't get a clear shot at the ones closest to you."

"Relax, I was teasing." Darlene sat down on the couch and stared at John-John. He was a younger image of his father, a few years older than her but in great physical shape. Under his gray T-shirt she could see his well-defined body, his arms popping out of his sleeves. He was built, and he was cute. She couldn't help stare at the bulge in his jeans. *What's wrong with me? Oh, yeah, I haven't been laid in months.*

"John-John and I share this house and the next one over. We use that one for supplies, weapons and such."

"John, please call me John." He shot a look at his father. "I haven't been John-John since I was twelve."

"You'll always be John-John." Murph stood. "It's time for bed. You kids get some rest as well. Big day tomorrow."

They both wished him a good night and John took his father's seat.

"What's tomorrow?" Darlene asked.

"What?"

"He said something about a big day tomorrow."

John laughed. "He says that every night. For thirty-five years I've been hearing that line."

He's thirty-five, Darlene thought, and made a mental note. Only seven years older and hot as Hell. She smiled.

"What's the matter?"

"What do you mean?" Darlene asked. She twirled her hair and tried to look casual when she took another swig of beer.

"Nothing." John rose. "I need to get some sleep. I actually have a big day ahead of me tomorrow. We're running low on supplies and I need to take a run up to St. Augustine and see if I can get some work or trade."

"Need company?"

John hesitated. "We'll see. Good-night. There are two vacant houses, so if you are planning on staying I'm sure Griff will let you have one."

"Who's Griff?"

"I'm sure you'll meet him tomorrow. Nothing much goes on without Griff and Peter and Kayla knowing. I'm sure they have a hundred questions for you."

Without another word John retired to a back bedroom.

Darlene was hoping for a seductive look, even a glance back when he walked out, but she got nothing. She heard his door close and heard the lock engage. She didn't blame him; these days the living were just as awful as the dead.

Darlene finished her beer and decided to slip into bed and think about her day until she passed out.

Chapter Nine

Darlene was disappointed but not surprised when she woke the next morning and saw that John had already left. Murph had a pot of coffee brewing and he was scrambling eggs. "Morning, missy," he said. "I hope you slept well."

"Haven't slept like that in, well, months. It sure beats sleeping in dumpsters and in abandoned houses."

"I would imagine." Murph slid some eggs onto two plates.

Darlene poured coffee for them and sat at the table. "How long have you lived here?"

"About four months."

"Really? I just assumed this had always been your home."

"Fat chance. These stilt houses go for close to a million bucks... well, they did before. When we got here this one was empty so we moved in. Pretty much everything you see was already here."

"Where are you from originally?"

"Pensacola. Born and raised in Florida." Murph forked some eggs. "I'm guessing from that accent that you're from either Boston or Rhode Island."

"A bit farther north. I'm from Maine. Born and raised, as they say."

"Ever been to Florida before all this?"

"No, I had never been farther south than Manhattan. How about you?"

"Never been farther than Virginia myself. I've never even seen snow in person."

"You haven't missed much. I just spent a winter buried in it in Baltimore and it was not fun."

"I'm getting too old to keep moving, but if I had a chance I'd love to go up there and see it before I die."

"If I never see another snowflake I'll be happy. If I never see the temperature dip below thirty-two I'll be happy as well." Darlene sipped her coffee. "God, how I miss having good coffee."

"That's the last of it for awhile, I'm afraid."

"Can we get more?" Darlene blurted. She felt foolish for saying it, like a spoiled brat.

"Eventually. It depends on what gets flown in and what we have to trade."

"John went to St. Augustine to get supplies?"

"Yes, and to trade if possible. We're running low on everything right now."

"I'm sorry." Darlene put her coffee mug down. "I thought you had enough food. I'm imposing."

"I always welcome the company. And I imagine you'll only be sticking around for a few days."

Darlene frowned. "Is my welcome over?"

Murph laughed. "Not at all. But most people that stumble upon us and don't want to raid us stay a few days before moving on to the safety of St. Augustine."

"Why don't you?"

Murph waved his hand. "I'm too damn old to climb down the ladder to this place. Damn near shit when I got up here. I'm actually afraid of heights. John does all of the running for the two of us and I inventory what we have, clean, cook, all of that. Truth be told I'm more of a burden to my kid."

"It sounds like you hold your own."

"I suppose." Murph winked. "I suppose you're just trying to be nice."

"Whatever." Darlene put the coffee mug to her lip but stopped.

"Something wrong?"

"The Sig Sauer."

"What about it?" Murph said and smiled. He patted his hip. "That's the longest in five years it's been away from me."

"I took it off of someone."

"I imagine that would be Carl."

"Lazy eye?"

"Yeah, that's Carl. He was only here for two days before he grabbed the gun, a box of food, the rest of the water, and my new pair of boots. Where is he now?"

"Near Hammond Beach."

"Doing what?" Murph said and grinned. "I'm guessing Carl didn't give you the Sig because you're so damn cute."

"Stranger things have happened, right?"

"I can't argue that." Murph pulled the weapon from his waistband and put it on the table. "It's actually yours now. You found it fair and square. My loss is your gain."

Darlene put a hand on the gun. "True. Thanks for giving it back."

Murph laughed. "This is actually the spot where you tell me, 'no, no, I can't separate a man from his prized weapon, you saved my life, you keep it.' Anything I'm saying make sense?"

"Nope." Darlene made to put the Sig Sauer in her own waistband. Laughing, she put it back on the table. "Just fucking with you, Murph."

"And a great sense of humor, too? God, what a package you are."

Darlene cleared the table when they were done. "Now what?"

"Now I usually sit and wait for him to return." Murph sat on the couch. "Want to watch a movie?"

"Seriously? I can't remember the last time I watched a movie, or heard a song, anything. This guy Jonathan, he was part of the Rear Guard, and I used to work with him and a couple of others. We'd watch the caravan from the back and make sure nothing snuck up on us, whether it was alive or dead. Jonathan had an MP3 player. He used to let me listen to songs when we were resting. Unfortunately the batteries died and he was always hoping to find more."

"Did he ever?"

Darlene sat down. "No. He died."

"He was one of them?"

"Yes, and it was my fault. I... I shot him, it was pure instinct. I..."

"You don't have to talk about it."

Darlene wiped a tear from her eye. "I'd rather not."

"Fair enough. Why don't you go and see if you like one of the movies?"

Darlene went to the DVD rack to the left of the plasma TV and browsed the titles. "I'm guessing a guy lived here."

"My kind of guy."

"John Wayne movies, Bruce Willis, Clint Eastwood, a ton of war movies, westerns, Charlton Heston, Stallone, Chuck Norris... not one chick flick."

"I threw those into the ocean."

Darlene shot him a dirty look.

"Just teasing, missy. I think this was some rich guy's Man Lair."

"His what?"

"I found not only all of these macho movies but a huge box of pornographic movies and magazines, as well as enough alcohol to inebriate Miami. There were guns, ammo, flak vests, an SUV and a couple of jet-ski's down below, and a drawer filled with various condoms and sexual devices. Whoever this guy was, he was a player, as the young kids say."

"Where's all that stuff now?"

Murph shrugged. "Most of it is worthless, to be realistic. I traded most of it away for food and water."

"You kept these shitty movies?"

"They are classics. Most of them, anyway. A man needs entertainment in these harsh times or he'd go stir crazy. We still have some of the alcohol, a case of rum somewhere."

"What about the guns? The SUV?"

173

"Worthless. I traded the guns and ammo for one of the bows John-John uses, and some clothes. Guns are too loud; they get the dead coming for miles with a single shot. The SUV and jet-skis were traded for a case of soda and fresh-cut meat. We ate steaks for a week."

"Got any left?"

"We don't have much left. I imagine we have another week of supplies for the three of us. Unless, of course, you move on."

"I don't think I'll be going anywhere for awhile, if that's alright with you. This is the first normal place I've been in since I can remember. No sense leaving just now, right? Besides, we have to watch every one of these shitty movies before I can go anywhere."

"I hear ya."

"How about we start with *Rocky* and then *Jaws*?"

"Fine with me. If I start to snore just kick me."

"Same goes for me."

Chapter Ten

Griff wasn't what Darlene expected. He was short, balding, with greasy hair and a greasy smile, pushing seventy. His clothes were unkempt and dirty, even though Darlene supposed he had access to a washer and dryer like Murph. Griff looked like his wardrobe and personal hygiene hadn't changed since the world went nuts.

Kayla, on the other hand, was in her forties and beautiful. Darlene wasn't into other women but she had to admire the way Kayla carried herself. The AK-47 in her strong hands didn't hurt, either. She wore a simple gray T-shirt, tight black jeans and Doc Marten boots. Her red hair was tied back and she wore no makeup. She was a natural beauty and didn't really need it. Darlene noticed a few freckles dotting her cheeks and nose.

"See anything you like?" Kayla said to Darlene as she shouldered the AK-47.

Darlene blushed and looked away. "Sorry."

"Don't be." Kayla winked. "You're pretty hot yourself."

Griff shot her a dirty look. "Enough with your lesbian bullshit for once. Every gal you see doesn't want to jump in bed with you."

"Not all, but some." Kayla smiled and licked her bottom lip. "Definitely this one."

"Thanks, but I prefer a man in my bed," Darlene said.

"Jesus." The other person before Darlene was Peter, and by his face it was obvious he was related to Griff and Kayla. He was pudgy around his middle but his arms were massive. His red-blonde hair flowed down his shoulders in curly locks, his face a bushy beard. "Can't we ever talk to chicks without you hitting on them?"

"Nope." Kayla patted him on the back. "Besides, you have no shot with this one, Petey. She's way out of your league."

Peter glanced at Darlene and then looked at his father for help. Griff just shrugged and spit tobacco juice over the edge of the deck. Darlene had gone to see Griff and his family just before dark. Murph had simply told her which stilt house.

"I'm too damn old to climb the ladder. Do me a favor, though, and ask Griff if he has any chewing tobacco. Tell him I'll pay him next time he comes up to see me," Murph said.

A day of lounging, watching movies and napping had put Darlene in a great frame of mind but she was sluggish. She could get used to this easy life and almost forget about the reality of what was going on not far from here, and all over the world.

"So…" Darlene said uneasily. Kayla was coming on way too strong; Peter was trying desperately to check out her ass and boobs without being caught, and so far Griff hadn't said much of anything.

Griff spit again and then opened the door. "Come on in and make yourself comfortable."

Darlene entered and smiled when she heard Griff tell his kids to stay outside. For emphasis he locked the door. "Have a seat. They'll come in through the backdoor in a bit. For now, we can talk in peace."

"Nice place you have here."

Griff shrugged. "It's not mine." He sat heavily in the chair and groaned. "I suppose it is mine now, but truth be told I wish I was back home in South Carolina preparing to die."

"That's an odd way of looking at it."

"I suppose you could make that argument." Griff pulled a small clear baggie from his pocket and tossed it to Darlene. "That's for Murph. Lord knows he pushed you over here for some chaw. Tell him he owes me."

"Will do."

Griff sat up in his chair. "Let's cut to the chase, because I'm not getting any younger. Why are you here?"

"I'm just trying to survive."

"Are you planning on going up to St. Augustine?"

"I hadn't planned anything. From the way Murph was talking I don't know if I have a real choice."

"What do you mean?" Griff pulled another baggie from his pocket and took a pinch, putting the tobacco in his mouth. "Everyone has a choice."

"He seemed like he was expecting me to split as soon as possible and head over to St. Augustine. I'm not even sure what's there."

"Civilization. Rebuilding. Electricity. When this started the people up there were smart enough to not just sit around and watch the boob tube and worry. They started blocking the roads, sealing off the main city from everything. The roads in and out were sandbagged and armed men and women patrolled them."

"Amazing."

"Not really, just smart. And they weren't the only ones to do so."

Darlene frowned. "What?"

"There are pockets, cities and towns and villages, all over the world, that have so far succeeded in fighting off the undead hordes. Places like Chicago, Austin, Boise, Cooperstown, Salt Lake City, Reading… the list goes on."

"How do you know that?"

"We get information from St. Augustine regularly. We act as their southern patrols and, in turn, they supply us with information and weapons to operate."

"Where else?"

"I know of a few small places that have survived. A place called Belford in New Jersey, the town of Falls River in Massachusetts, somewhere called Dexter, Maine –"

"You're a liar," Darlene blurted. "You can't know that."

"All I can do is pass along the information."

"Dexter was aflame when I left."

"From what I understand, after the harsh winter past, they were able to rebuild and fortify the roads in and out. The undead up there froze in place. It was easy to chop them down like trees."

Darlene folded in the chair. Was it possible? Had she run so far, hundreds and hundreds of miles, to escape the zombies, when all she had to do was stay at home?

"From reports, it was touch and go for many. About ninety-five percent of the population was killed. You made the right choice leaving."

"It doesn't feel like it."

"You're still alive."

"While everything I knew, everyone I loved is dead. Or are they?"

Griff shrugged. "Who knows? You very likely might be dead right now if you'd stayed. Perhaps someone you loved would have had to kill you by now."

Darlene was feeling overwhelmed and switched the subject before she started to cry. "I'd like to stay here for a while, if that's alright with you."

"I don't have a problem with it. As long as Murph says it's alright. I can get you the keys for one of the empty houses tomorrow. You'll be on your own as far as food, furniture and weapons are concerned. I'm sure everyone will pitch in and help you out. Any skills you have will be appreciated as well."

The backdoor opened.

"Time to leave. It was nice to meet you," Griff said. "Forgive me if I don't see you down, but I'm too damn old for that."

Chapter Eleven

John held up a finger, staring at Darlene.

"God, just ask me out already," she whispered.

He waved his hand for her to be quiet. Darlene covered her mouth to stifle a smile and a laugh. When you were out here, with John and a compound bow, you took it seriously.

Two walking corpses were directly below them, shuffling aimlessly on the road. They were both wearing the tattered remains of police officers, holstered guns still at their sides.

John pointed two fingers at Darlene and they both notched an arrow to their bow. She stared down the shaft at the zombie on the left and aimed right between his eyes.

A low grunt from John was the signal and they let fly at the same time. John's zombie took the arrow in his forehead, and he fell silently to the ground.

Darlene's arrow shot high and wide left, missing by at least five feet. Before she could pull another arrow out, John had already fired a second and the arrow ripped through the zombie's left eye, putting him down.

"Shit," she murmured.

John looked aggravated but didn't say a word. Instead he put his bow down, pulled a Bowie knife, and slid down the sand dune. Darlene, embarrassed, followed. This was her third day in a row out with John looking for supplies. So far they'd encountered dozens of the undead, nothing salvageable, and she still hadn't hit a target.

"Can't I just use my machete? I can't even count how many I've killed with this thing."

"It's a close-range weapon. What do you do when there are fifteen of them surrounding you?"

"Swing for the fences," Darlene replied.

"I'm amazed you're still alive."

"Lucky, I guess." Darlene stood watch as John removed the service pistols, extra ammo, two dead walkie-talkies and handcuffs from the two expired cops.

"With any luck there'll be a squad car around here with a shotgun and a trunk filled with supplies."

"Which way?" Darlene asked.

"We can cut through and get to a main highway."

"Have you been out this way before?"

"Not really. I've picked the peninsula from Anastasia Island to Ormond-by-the-Sea clean over the last twelve months. There isn't much left but sand and zombies."

"I beg to differ."

John stopped. "What do you mean?"

"I found a spot filled with bottles of water."

"You're lying."

"And you're rude." In the last three days John had been gruff and short with Darlene. He'd spent most of his time in the stilt house in his room with the door closed. Murph said that John had a wife and two young children, and he'd been looking for them. Their bodies hadn't been found, but the chance that they were living was small. Despite trying to be nice to John – for the sake of getting along and because, honestly, he was a hunk – Darlene wasn't getting too far with him. Murph had suggested that Darlene earn her keep and learn to shoot, but so far it was backfiring. John had even pled with his father this morning to let him go by himself.

"Where is this magical land of bottled water?" John said sarcastically.

"Forget it." Darlene started walking away. "I'll just save that card up my sleeve for the next guy that comes along. Maybe he won't be such a fucking dick."

"Nice mouth."

"Nice attitude. Do you always treat women this shitty?"

John grabbed her arm and stopped her.

He was on the ground, his back and head slamming to the sand, before he could catch his breath.

"Don't put your fucking hands on me, got it?" Darlene shook her head and stepped away before she attacked him again. She could feel the anger in her, coursing through her body like a spring. She was ready to snap.

"Got it. Loud and clear." John stood and brushed himself off, face red in embarrassment. "I am sorry. It's just that..."

"Don't worry about it. Let's just keep moving before we're surrounded."

John put up a hand in protest but Darlene was already twenty feet from him, moving quickly onto a zombie that had appeared. She drew her machete and chopped into its thick neck, driving it backwards. A second cut and its head fell to the sand.

"I don't need this," Darlene said and put the compound bow and arrows on the ground. She shook the machete. "I'd rather die with this in my hand than try to work with that. Sorry."

"Not a problem." John picked up the equipment. "You're a pretty shitty shot, anyway." He put on his best smile.

"Whatever." Darlene turned away again. She hoped he would think she was being a bitch and not forgiving him, but the reality was that his smile melted her. She didn't want to see her return smile.

"We can cut through these side streets and we'll emerge onto Route 1. With any luck the cop car will be there."

They kept to the middle of the street as they moved from the beachside to a totaled neighborhood. The only bodies were charred and unmoving, the houses rotting and scorched. John explained that he'd ransacked this area a few months ago.

"What were you before this?" Darlene asked as they got to the end of the street and pushed through a debris-strewn field. They could see Route 1 ahead.

"I was a cop in Tallahassee. I was doing my rounds when this… thing happened to everyone. I was across town. My wife and girls were home. I shot my way through miles of undead before getting there."

"What happened?"

"They were gone. Packed and left. The ironic part is that the zombies hadn't even gotten to that part of town yet. I packed some food, my extra weapons and ammo, and drove to my father's house. He was ready to go. We went in search of them."

Darlene and John emerged onto a deserted highway. "There's the cop car," she said.

They approached cautiously, watching both sides of the road for movement. Just beyond the squad car a pickup truck had flipped across the southbound lane, wedging at least six cars behind it. John pointed to the pileup. They couldn't see anything moving, but to the outside were thick woods.

John had an arrow notched and ready to fire. As they drew closer he put it away and drew his knife again. Darlene had the machete out.

They moved in opposite directions to get around the squad car. Both doors were opened, which wasn't a good sign. Darlene checked the woods one more time. Empty. Quiet. The hair on the back of her neck rose like in a bad horror movie. She wanted to throw up as she rounded the car and leveled the machete at the open door.

John was on the other side, but there was no one in the car. No blood, no gore, no body parts. "Shotgun," he said and climbed into the passenger side. "And a box of shells. Sweet."

Darlene relaxed and leaned against the car. "Now what?"

"The keys are in it."

"So?"

"So we drive this baby as far back as we can and then go home. It's been too long since I've driven one."

"Who says you can drive?" Darlene went to climb into the car but John was already in the driver's seat and smiling. He turned the key and it began to click.

"So much for that idea."

"Not really. It isn't completely dead. I bet I can get her started. She's been sitting out here for months." John popped the hood and got out. "Get in and I'll tell you when to start it."

Darlene jumped in. "Sure, but don't expect me to move over. I'm the driver, I own the road."

John laughed and raised the hood, peering around it at Darlene. "Don't do anything until I tell you."

"You got it." Darlene could hear a crow in the distance. She wondered why animals hadn't been affected by the virus, or the plague, or whatever this really was. Maybe Murph knew the answer. She had so many questions for him but never found the time to ask, too content to sit and relax and watch movies.

The last three days had been the best days in too long, sharing conversation, food and company with another human being. Darlene wondered how many days, weeks or even months between actual conversations she'd had. Besides whispering to herself, of course. "I wonder if I'm crazy," she murmured.

"What?" John asked from under the hood. "Did you say something?"

"Just wondering what's taking so damn long."

"Give me a second. Patience is a virtue."

Darlene laughed. "Whatever."

John poked his head around the hood and grinned. "Try it."

Darlene turned the key and the car hesitated, trying to turn over. For a second she thought it would but it went back to clicking.

"The belt is loose. Without tools I can't fix it. Pop the trunk." John went around and fished through the trunk. "He actually had tools."

"Is that a big deal?" Darlene asked, getting out and stretching her legs. A quick look around told her they were still alone.

"For a cop car? Hell yeah. Everyone knows that you don't leave shit in a cop car, especially personal items." John slid under the front of the car.

"Cops stealing from cops. What's wrong with that picture?"

"That's reality sometimes. You can't trust anyone," John said.

Darlene got back in and sat down, rubbing her eyes. It was hot today, like every other Florida day. She started to hum a Tori Amos tune and wondered if Tori was wandering around California or New York trying to eat people.

"Try it again."

Darlene turned the key. The engine stuttered but then roared to life.

"Told you I could do it," John said and slammed the hood closed. "Move over, I'm driving."

"John, get in the car. Now."

"Not until you move over."

"Get in the fucking car." Darlene drew her Desert Eagle and fired just over John's shoulder.

John turned just as seven zombies came within ten feet of them. A glance in the rearview mirror and Darlene held her breath. There were ten coming up behind her and more wandering in from the woods.

Chapter Twelve

The first zombie Darlene slammed into with the car landed on the hood. Darlene screamed and pissed herself.

"Left! Left!" John yelled. "Shoot for that gap."

Route 1 was flooded with slow-moving undead, obstacles drawn to the speeding car. She was only doing thirty as she hit the second and third and forth, the car fishtailing as she bump-bumped over the bodies. Unlike movies, hitting them was slowing her down and she knew it was only a matter of time before she lost control of the car and ended up in a ditch.

They appeared like ants from either side of the road, an endless stream of corpses. Darlene wondered aloud why there were so many.

"We're close to the outskirts of St. Augustine right now. We're trapped between the barriers of the city and these creatures now. There might be hundreds, thousands of them out here." John wiped sweat from his brow. "Just keep driving."

Darlene hit another two zombies, two smaller children, and felt the car lurch to her right. She overcorrected and the car spun out. Her chest slammed into the steering wheel, jarring her.

"Are you alright?" John asked.

"Sure." She lifted her gun and pulled the trigger, just in front of his face, as John covered his ears. The shot, through the opened passenger window, missed her mark. "You drive."

"What?"

Darlene got out of the car, firing at anything close enough to get to them. She ran around the car and slipped into the passenger side. John slid over the seat, threw the car in gear and floored it, immediately running over three undead.

A mile away, after barreling through ten more undead blocking the path, the road opened up. Single stray zombies crossed their path and it was easy for John to skirt around them.

"Up ahead is the 207 bridge. We should cross back over there instead of running north into another cluster of them," John said. "It feels good to drive again."

"Yeah, the three minutes I drove were exciting." Darlene laughed. "My hands are shaking."

"My hands always shake, if that's any consolation."

They turned onto Route 207, the gas station and restaurant a smoldering pile of rubble at the entrance. Zombies lurched around the structures but they were too far away to be a threat.

"We need to be very careful when we get out."

"Why are we getting out?" Darlene asked but then saw why. The 207 bridge had been barricaded on this side with a pile of damaged cars, a makeshift fence of wood and metal, and chunks of cement.

John parked right in front of the barrier. "Watch either side when we get out."

They emerged and went to the wall, John searching frantically. "There's a path hidden up here somewhere. I was told that once you get onto the bridge you can safely cross."

A fence had also been erected to either side of the bridge, following the waterline. Zombies were pulling themselves from the water and throwing themselves against the hurdle.

Darlene trained her Desert Eagle on the road they'd just come from, but it was empty. *So far so good. With any luck we'll be across and closer to home before they come.* Darlene didn't like the fact that trees covered both sides of the road. There could be a horde a few feet away and she wouldn't know it. She checked her ammo. Murph had surprised her with two clips for the Desert Eagle, for which she was grateful.

"I think I found it."

"It's about time," Darlene said sarcastically. Every second out here, exposed with their backs to the proverbial wall was a mistake. "Lead the way."

"I just need to push this block out of the way. You can see the path behind it. I think I need your help," John said.

Darlene glanced down the road one more time and did a double-take. "They're here."

A score of zombies had emerged from the left side of the road, pushing through the underbrush and from between the trees. Further down, near the turnoff to 207, she could see a dozen more catching up.

"We have about five minutes before we're attacked, just so you know." Darlene didn't want to start shooting and draw more attention to them. Five more undead appeared from the other side of the road and started toward them. "Talk to me."

"I can't get it." John was sweating as he tugged on the cement block barring their path. "You need to help me."

"I think you need to help me. They're getting too close." Before Darlene could point and fire John was already moving past her with an arrow notched to the bow.

The two closest zombies were put down in quick succession. "Don't fire unless they get within six feet of me. I can take them out at a farther range. Just feed me arrows until we can clear a zone."

John began cutting them down, bombarding the undead with arrows to the head. Darlene had to admit that she was impressed. One came from their left and almost got to them before Darlene saw him and put the Desert Eagle almost to his forehead before shooting.

"That was too close for comfort," she said.

"I agree." John had cleared them within twenty feet but more now stalked from the woods. "There might be a hundred. I don't have enough arrows and you don't have enough bullets."

"What do we do?"

"Start shooting. If we can clear them another twenty feet we might have time to get the cement moved."

"I hope so." Darlene began picking them off, concentrating on the left-hand side while John went to work on the right.

"This is hopeless," John said. For every one they dropped another two now took its place, coming out of the woods from only fifteen feet away on either side.

They kept at it. Darlene finished her clip and put in a new one, wondering if this would be the last one she'd ever have and wondering if she should save two bullets for them.

She hadn't told John or Murph about survivors in Maine. Her goal was to stay here through the summer and winter, build up her strength and supplies and then head north. She knew that patience was not her strong suit but she didn't want to risk another winter in the northeast. Now she wished she'd told John and Murph of her plan. Somehow she felt like she'd eventually be abandoning them, even though she owed nothing real to them and them to her. Still…

John fired his last arrow a second before her pistol was empty. They immediately turned and fumbled with the cement block. They'd managed to clear a thirty foot zone before them but the zombies would close it soon enough.

The cement block moved a few inches and John was able to get his hands under it. "Push it," he yelled, trying to keep the weight from falling and crushing his hands.

When the machine gun fire started he almost dropped it.

"Who the fuck is that?" Darlene asked.

A figure, dressed in black, face covered in a black hood, was sitting on a Harley Davidson shooting an M4 assault rifle. He tossed a grenade into the tree line.

"We're saved," Darlene said.

"No. That's Azrael." John worked frantically to move the block. "If we don't move this he'll shoot us dead as quick as he'll shoot zombies."

The grenade went off in the woods.

"Shit." Darlene put her back into it to lift the cement block as a bullet bounced off of the fence next to her.

Chapter Thirteen

They got the cement block off to the side and John stepped over it, reaching back to help Darlene. "Behind you!" he shouted.

She turned, pulling her machete and cutting with it in one motion. An arm from the nearest undead flew into the water. She began hacking at its neck and on the third slice it severed.

"Let's go, he's still firing!" John urged her.

Darlene kicked another zombie back into the pack, who now pushed to get at her. The sound of bullets hitting zombies and ricocheting off of the asphalt was making her shake and she tried to duck and fight at the same time.

"Now!" John finally said. "He'll shoot us both."

She took one wide swing and cut into another neck before jumping back and over the cement block.

"Help me push it back!" John said as he gripped it again and put his shoulder into it. Darlene joined him, a bullet ricocheting just past her chin. It was easier to push it back into place and despite the hands trying to reach over and grab them they managed to set it so it couldn't be moved.

"Run," John said and began moving across the bridge, which was completely empty of debris, cars or bodies.

Darlene followed close behind, marveling at how odd it was to have found such refuge amidst all of the chaos. You could put your head down and imagine cars coming up behind you, tourists roaring toward the beaches. To either side the river lapped at the pylons, another lazy summer day.

The sound of gunfire receding in the distance broke her from the spell. When they got halfway over the bridge they stopped.

Another explosion rocked the trees, and they watched as smoke and fire billowed near the bridge, a tree dropping into the river.

"Was he throwing grenades?" Darlene asked.

"Yeah." John put his hands on his knees and tried to catch his breath. Finally he sat down in the middle of the bridge. "He won't follow us."

"Are you sure?"

"Not really." John put his head down on the sun-baked asphalt and stretched his legs.

"What are you doing?"

"Enjoying a nap. Grab it while you can."

"You're not serious."

"Damn serious. Where else, besides back home, will you ever be safe? There's no way the zombies can get to us."

"What about ... whatever his name is on the bike?" Darlene sat down next to him.

"If he wants to he'll shoot us long distance. I'm not worried about him. I'm worried about the noise we created and the dozens of zombies amassing on the eastern end of the bridge."

"Who is he?"

"I told you. Azrael."

"Like the bad cat in the Smurfs cartoon?"

John laughed. "As in the Angel of Death."

Darlene shrugged. "I think the old guy from the cartoon was worse."

"Papa Smurf?"

"Forget it." Darlene stood back up and brushed off her pants. "Who is he?"

"Some lunatic. He's been around for a few months. He sets all of these roadblocks and traps. When we sent someone to talk to him he started shooting. Now we just stay clear of him and he inadvertently helps us with his work. That place that we met? He set all of that up; I just use it to kill them."

"You mean the place where you tried to kill me?"

"Not quite. If I wanted to I would have killed you."

Darlene laughed and playfully nudged him with her foot. "I'm too fast a target for you. I'm like a panther."

"Really? I could've easily hit those boobs of yours."

"Pervert," Darlene said and went to kick him harder this time. John grabbed her foot and yanked her. She fell onto him and he circled her in a bear hug.

"You were saying?" he whispered in her ear.

Darlene immediately reacted in two very different ways: her body stiffened at his touch, so unused to physical contact that was not violent; and she also got wet. "Get off of me," she said and rolled her eyes when her voice quivered. She wanted him inside of her, right here on the bridge, Azrael and zombies be damned.

"Sorry." John pulled away from her and sat up. He turned his head away from her. "I got carried away."

"It's alright. Just two adults having some fun, right?"

"I'm married," he finally said.

"I know." Darlene stood and walked over to the edge, looking down at the water. "It's just..."

"We should get going if we're going to get home before dark." John took a few steps away from Darlene.

"Is she out there?" Darlene asked.

"Yes. Somewhere she's alive and waiting for me. She's safe and right now laughing with my daughters."

"I hope so."

John turned and eyed her, his eyes swollen. "I can feel her, like she's sending me messages or something."

Darlene nodded. She really did hope for his sake that they were alive, no matter how remote the chance was. "Where's your uniform?" she asked, changing the subject.

"What uniform?" John asked and turned back the way they'd come. "I think he left. I don't hear gunfire or explosions."

"That's good."

"The problem will be getting past the ones that were alerted on the other side by all of the noise. I hope we gave them enough time to get bored and move along."

"Uniform," Darlene said as she started walking.

"I still don't get it."

"You told me you were a cop. In every horror movie, especially zombie movies, the hero has a heart of gold, a knowing smile, and a cop uniform on."

"Sorry. After a year I decided to retire the uniform and put on more comfortable clothes."

"The uniform would have been better. It would give you that authority, that sense of righteous purpose."

John snickered. "I already have a sense of righteous purpose."

"Any idea what that is?"

"Not a clue." John laughed. "But it sounds pompous. I like it."

"I thought you would. And next time you talk about my tits I'll shoot you."

"As long as it's with a bow, I'll be safe."

"Fuck you," Darlene said and missed with a punch.

"You wish."

You have no idea, Darlene thought and tried to concentrate on walking next to him.

Chapter Fourteen

There was a soft thud on the stairs below her new house. Darlene drew her Desert Eagle, always on her side, and walked quietly to the front door. Someone or something was coming up the steps unannounced, a great way to get a bullet between the eyes.

She opened the door and trained the weapon on the top of the stairs.

Another step and then nothing. "Hello?" a female voice called up. "Are you home?"

"Bitch." Darlene went to the stairs and looked down. Kayla was coming up the steps holding a picnic basket. Her white T-shirt was tight across her bra-less chest and tied under it, revealing her taut stomach and pierced bellybutton.

"I'm just bringing you a housewarming present."

"A picnic basket?" Darlene asked, trying not to stare as Kayla came up and stood next to her. *I'm not a fucking lesbian, but she is sexy.* Darlene wanted to slap the thought from her head.

"No, me, silly." Kayla laughed. "This is just for after, when we're hungry."

"I've already explained myself." Darlene couldn't help the edge in her voice. Kayla might be beautiful but she was also so damn arrogant.

"I'm just teasing. I brought a bottle of wine, some fresh cheese and crackers. Peter went into St. Augustine yesterday and I asked him to pick me up a few things."

"That is kind," Darlene said. "Won't you come in?"

The house was a mess. Griff had decided after Darlene and John came back and told of the run-in with Azrael that she needed her own place to relax for a couple of days before deciding what she wanted to do. She knew what she wanted to do: stay for a few months, gather supplies, weapons and information, and then head back north to home. For now, this would be her home.

Most of the furniture was very expensive and very gaudy. The woman of the house – the owners were a middle-aged couple of obvious wealth – had made it very feminine, with gold trim, seraph ornaments, light colored rooms and muted amber hues on the upholstery. There were doilies and covers on almost everything. The family had owned horses, and there were statues, plaques and photos adorning every room in the house save for the back room.

The back room was the man's cave, filled with football memorabilia, a sixty-inch plasma television, surround sound, and a vast pornography collection. Darlene had wasted no time in rummaging through the DVD's in hope of finding something to take her mind off of things, but it was exclusively lesbian videos, and most of them of the group variety.

"It looks like the Soprano's threw up in here," Kayla blurted.

Darlene couldn't help but laugh. "Yeah, they were definitely from New York or New Jersey. The guy has a room full of New York Jets crap. Want any of it?"

"Any baseball bats? We could always use weapons." Kayla set the basket on the kitchen table as she moved through the rooms. "It could use some work, but nothing a garbage can couldn't solve. I see they liked horses."

"You could say that. I keep expecting to open up an extra bedroom and finding a zombie horse or something."

"That would be fun. I'm sure we'll be happy here together," Kayla said.

"No fucking –"

"Wow, are you easy to rile up. I'm just busting your chops. Relax. I promise to not make you uncomfortable, as long as you stop staring at my tits. Is that fair?"

Darlene blushed and looked away. "No idea what you're talking about, but not a problem." Darlene went back into the kitchen and began unloading the basket.

Kayla came in and opened the cabinet, procuring two wine glasses. "These are probably worth a grand a piece." She sat down at the table.

"Worthless now." Darlene put the cheese and crackers onto a tray.

"Not really. Trust me, there's always someone who wants what they haven't got. Most of this junk here could be brought to the city and traded for perishables. There's a market for just about anything."

"The only thing I need short-term is new clothes. A nice, comfortable pair of jeans, some sneakers that fit, a pack of socks, a bra that doesn't make my girls bounce when I run from zombies, and some panties."

"You strike me as a g-string kinda gal," Kayla said and grinned.

Darlene couldn't help but smile. "You said you'd play nice."

"You haven't stopped looking at them yet." Kayla sat up in her chair. "Say the word and this shirt comes off."

"Pour the wine." Darlene went to the drawer and got a knife for the cheese. "And I prefer thongs."

'I prefer nothing. It's easier to bury your face that way."

"You're sick." Darlene cut the cheese into squares and placed them on a plate, fixing the crackers in a nice pattern. "Lunch is served."

Kayla sipped at the wine and ignored the food.

"Aren't you going to eat?" Darlene asked around a mouthful of cheese and crackers.

"I ate before I came over. This is for you." Kayla tapped on a wine bottle. "I'm going to do a liquid lunch today. Won't you join me?"

'I think I might," Darlene said with a laugh. She raised her glass. "A toast."

Kayla lifted hers. "A toast to what?"

"Life."

"And still being alive." Kayla tapped her glass against Darlene's and finished hers in one gulp. She quickly refilled her glass.

"You'll get drunk that way."

"That's the idea." Kayla pointed at Darlene's glass. "Keep up."

"I don't think so." Darlene put a hunk of cheese into her mouth.

"Suit yourself." Kayla sipped her wine and sat back. "Let's talk about nothing of consequence for a bit." She glanced out the window. "It's a beautiful day today, isn't it?"

"It's another sunny, hot day. I never thought I'd pray for rain, but it would be great to break the days apart." Darlene finished her glass and smiled when Kayla poured her another one. "This is my last one."

Three glasses later the bottle was empty and they'd retired to the living room, stretched out on the couch. Darlene was feeling great, giddy and light-headed. She tried to stand but fell down onto Kayla with a laugh. "I need to pee," she slurred.

"I think you need to relax first." Kayla helped her sit up next to her. "Close your eyes."

Darlene's eyes grew wide. Even in her drunken stupor she had some senses working. "I don't want this."

"Want what?" Kayla said and stroked Darlene's face with her fingers, tracing her chin. "I would never do anything that you didn't want."

Darlene closed her eyes and relaxed. The wine was making her feel good and free. For the first time in forever she didn't worry about being bitten or being raped or being ripped apart. She only felt... horny, if she were being honest with herself. Would it be so bad to make love to Kayla? She was beautiful. *You could do a lot worse than her,* Darlene thought. Under normal circumstances she wouldn't even dream of this, but there was nothing normal about anything.

Darlene leaned forward and puckered her lips.

Kayla held her close and Darlene could feel her breath in her ear. "I would love nothing more than to have you, to taste every part of you, to make you cum." Kayla kissed her softly on the cheek. "I'll see you tomorrow."

Darlene opened her eyes confused. "You're leaving?"

"Trust me, it's for the better."

"I don't think so."

Kayla put a hand on Darlene's arm and let it linger. "I do. Go get some food into your system."

As Kayla left Darlene went to a cabinet and pulled out a bottle of Grey Goose. *I'll get some more drink into me, thank you very much.*

Chapter Fifteen

Darlene woke up to the sound of pouring rain. Her head felt like someone had run it over and she swore that she would never drink wine again. Her stomach lurched as she struggled out of the bed, eye on the bathroom door. 'Please let me make it," she whispered.

She didn't. She crumbled in the doorway of the bathroom and spewed her stomach contents on the floor. Closing her eyes, she swore that she'd never drink another drop of alcohol.

The rain stopped midmorning, jarring a stiff Darlene from the floor. Her head still hurt and her sides felt like she'd been kicked in the ribs. She had no idea how long she'd been unconscious. The smell of the floor and her clothes made her gag.

Getting to the couch took her twenty minutes, her limbs refusing to work for her. She was so exhausted by the time she hit the cushions that she closed her eyes and fell back asleep.

A knock at the door jarred her awake, a stabbing pain in her forehead. "Go away," she tried to say but her throat was so dry that she simply made a squeaking noise. At this point, if it were a horde of zombies, she'd gladly let them eat her. Anything to stop the pain.

"Darlene?"

It was John. He knocked again. "Are you alright?"

Darlene glanced down at her stained shirt and sighed. She put her fingers through her hair and came away with something gray and sticky. She had to laugh, but knew it would hurt.

John knocked on the door again.

"Come in," she finally managed. As the door opened – she was so glad that it was unlocked and she didn't have to spend an hour trying to rise and unlock it – she propped herself on a couch pillow with an elbow and tried to smile. *Maybe he won't notice how I look, or how I smell.*

John stopped in his tracks. "Oh my God, are you alright?"

"Sure."

"You look like..."

"Shit?" she finally said.

"Well, yeah," John said and sat down on a chair across from her. He made a face. "What is that smell?"

"Crackers, cheese and wine." Darlene felt her stomach roiling again. "I might need some help to the bathroom."

John rose and helped her slowly to her feet. They moved gingerly to the bathroom. "Let's try to hit the toilet bowl this time," John said and stepped over the explosion in the doorway.

"Hold my hair back," Darlene said and dropped to the floor, her face buried in the bowl.

"This is how most of my dates in high school ended," John quipped.

Despite the situation and the rising bile in her throat Darlene laughed.

"Of course, it was awkward the next day in class when she would tell everyone about holding my hair back while I puked."

"You are quite the comedian," Darlene said before emptying what was left of her stomach into the water. Three gags later and she was finished for now.

"Let's get you back into bed. Is there any way you can change yourself?" John asked.

"None whatsoever." Darlene was getting sicker just by smelling her clothes. "If you promise to not ravish me, I'll let you strip me."

"I promise." He lifted her up off of the floor and carried-dragged-shuffled her to the bedroom.

Darlene put her face near his and smiled. "Of course, once all of this is over, feel free to ravish me."

John grimaced. "Your breath could knock a buzzard off of a shit wagon." He put her at arm's length, made sure she was balanced, and stripped off her shirt.

"See anything you like?" Darlene asked. She knew she was being silly but she was getting very self-conscious and very embarrassed.

"Nothing sexier than a girl covered in puke."

Darlene put her hands on her hips and was proud that she didn't fall over. She exaggerated a pout with her bottom lip. "Are you saying I'm ugly?"

John shook his head, looked away from her, and unbuttoned her pants. "I'm not saying that at all."

"Then you think I'm ugly?"

John got her pants down to her ankles and she stepped out of them. She caught him glancing quickly at the front of her blue thongs.

"Get into bed. Can you manage that?" John said.

"Care to join me?" Darlene said as she crawled onto the bed and put her ass in the air. "See anything you like?"

John's face grew red and he turned away. "I have to go."

"Do you really?" Despite being weak and sick she wanted him. She knew she was being stupid and desperate but she didn't care.

John stared into her eyes. "I'm married."

Darlene had nothing to say to that. "I'm sorry," she finally whispered and got under the covers.

"I'll see you later." John turned and walked away.

"Wait, John."

"Yes?" John didn't even turn as he stopped.

"I'm really, really sorry. Please come back in a few hours and check on me. Please."

"I will."

Chapter Sixteen

"Feeling better?"

"Much." Darlene was standing on the porch, overlooking the Atlantic Ocean. She held a glass of water in her hands. "I needed a few more hours of sleep, I guess."

John leaned on the rail. "You were a mess."

"Thanks." Darlene sipped at the cold water. "I appreciate you reminding me of that." She stared at John. "And thanks for coming back and checking up on me, and for putting me into bed in the first place." Darlene looked back to the ocean. "I'm really sorry for what I said, that was so stupid of me."

"Forget it."

"I can't. I was being selfish and stupid."

"You were being human."

Darlene shook her head. "I hope we can still be friends."

John put a tentative hand on her shoulder. "Of course we can still be friends."

"Good. I'll never bring it up again."

"Fair enough. Besides, now I know how you feel about me." John smiled and winked. "It's obvious you have a crush on me."

"You dick."

The sky was clear in the fading light of day, the heat shimmering off of the sand surrounding them. No trace of the rains remained. *Welcome to Florida,* she thought.

"Can I ask you a personal question?" John said slowly.

"Yes, they are real." She squeezed her chest.

John laughed. "Are you always so forward?"

"Is that your question?"

"My first question."

"I never was before. I was always very shy, if you can believe that. I grew up in a very small and very close-knit little town in Maine. I was the ugly duckling growing up."

"I doubt that."

"It's true. I didn't have a boyfriend until my senior year, and that ended horribly. My father worked in factories all of his life. My father actually helped manufacture the Desert Eagle I carry. He gave that gun to me on my sixteenth birthday and taught me how to shoot it."

"Do you think he's still alive?"

Darlene looked him in the eyes. "I killed him with the Desert Eagle when he turned."

"Sorry."

"Not your fault. Anyway, that feels like a hundred years ago. I've been through so much in the last few months. Hell, I've been through so much in the last few weeks and days. I'm sometimes amazed that I haven't simply collapsed and given up."

"I feel the same way. For me the motivation to see my wife and kids keeps me going." John grew quiet and stared into the darkness creeping over the water.

Darlene figured that she'd give him some room and not broach the subject again. It was obvious after this morning and his words and body language now that it was all still fresh in his mind. He'd never gotten over the fact that he was here and they were somewhere else. And more than likely dead or worse right now.

"I know it's such a long shot that they are alive. My dad keeps trying to change the subject when I bring them up. It's like that time that the little boy went missing in the mall and the mother was on TV pleading with his abductor to return him safely. Three weeks later she was still on the news, crying and ranting, for the safe return of her son. We all knew the truth. We knew her son was beyond help and wouldn't return to her alive." John rubbed his eyes.

"I don't remember that, but the story is common enough."

"It happened at the mall where I worked in Tallahassee. A month later they found his body. It was buried in six inches of mud a half a mile behind the mall. They'd scoured that area for days and days without finding him. The autopsy confirmed that he had been killed within hours of the kidnapping."

"That's awful." Darlene didn't know what else to say.

"Yes, it is. But his mom had hope, whether it was realistic or not. I have to have hope, don't I?"

"Of course you do. You need that to keep going, to get up every day and face the terror that has become our existence. I commend you for that."

John glanced at Darlene and smiled. "Now, for my real question."

"Shoot."

John pointed at her ankle. "Want to tell me about that bite and why you're still alive?"

Darlene squirmed and her first instinct was to get up and go inside. Unconsciously she scratched at the dark mark on her ankle under her sock. "How do you know? Don't tell me you stripped me completely down this morning. How embarrassing."

"Not at all, although I did get to see you without a shirt and pants."

Darlene put her head down and feigned embarrassment. "Great."

"My dad told me about it the day you showed up here. He said it didn't look that fresh, although it was still raw-looking and the blood just under the skin was black. He thought for sure you'd turn any minute, but you never did."

"Why didn't he say anything?"

"I think he was just happy to see you still alive. It was obvious that you had no symptoms."

"I don't really want to talk about it." Darlene covered her ankle with her hand. "Not yet. I still have nightmares."

"Fair enough."

Darlene turned to John and grinned. "I thought you said you were a cop."

John hesitated. "I am."

"A mall cop?"

"It's still a cop."

Darlene laughed. "And all this time I thought I was being protected by this hardcore police officer. I put my life in the hands of a guy who chases skateboarders from the parking lot."

"Ouch."

"The guy who gets a discount in the food court."

"Stop," John said and tried not to laugh. "You call me mean."

"The guy who drives around the parking lot at nine-fifteen at night to make sure the makeup girls and stock boys get to their car safely."

"You're killing me. What did you do for a living?"

"I was a makeup girl in a mall."

"Not funny."

Darlene slapped the deck. "I wish I were joking."

Chapter Seventeen

Darlene, John and a dozen others moved quickly down A1A, clearing a path through the zombies coming from the south. Bridgette Charland, fourteen and preferring to be called Bri, carried John's extra arrows slung over her shoulders. It was obvious to everyone that she had a massive crush on him.

Six hours ago a broken CB radio transmission had announced from one of the southern safe spots near Daytona Beach that a flood of refugees were coming east and north from Orlando. The city, twice the size of St. Augustine, had collapsed under its own weight and with so many zombie attacks.

"There's a spiked pit to the left," someone called out. They were entering Flagler Beach and the junction of Route 100. At some point this had been a central point for survivors. Now it was desolate. Traps and ditches had been built to either side of the road and the beach littered with fencing, makeshift walls and abandoned cars.

While the group took a quick break and no undead were in the immediate vicinity, Darlene accompanied three men inside a restaurant called the Golden Lion, its wind-faded sign a regal lion. The bar area was covered in sand, as the glass partitions had been destroyed. The kitchen yielded nothing worth taking, the food stores emptied.

Darlene went slowly up the stairs to the top deck of the place. She imagined how beautiful this would have been in times past, with the drinks and good food, company, the wind blowing in your hair and the smell of the surf and sand. She stared at the beach, covered in debris, and imagined sunbathers, children frolicking in the waves, lifeguards in their chairs, some Jimmy Buffet music playing from a small radio.

"John says we're ready to head out." Bri stood at the head of the stairs. She looked so young, too young to be out here in danger. Darlene supposed there was nothing but danger, no matter where you were. She wanted to say something soothing to the girl. She couldn't think of anything to say that wouldn't be condescending to the teen.

They went back out into the street and got back into formation. Darlene took the sweep to the far right with her machete while John was to the left, arrow notched. So far the zombies had been light, with months of fortifying the few bridges that remained to the peninsula. Farther south, near Ormond Beach and Daytona Beach it would be a different story unless an unknown group of survivors had staked a claim there.

"Just up ahead is where our reach stops. There's a state park around a bend and we were able to pull a group of RV's into the road and build a wall. The beach in that spot has also been fenced in, and the park has a natural rock wall that we added to. After that it could get messy," Eric White said. He was an older man that used to be in construction and had built quite a bit of the traps and walls in this area. His long, white ponytail dripped down his back, sweat running off onto his shirtless chest. He carried a hand crossbow that he was quite proud of, having found it in a junk pile and fashioned it back to working condition. Darlene thought someone had once said that Eric had been a consultant on one of those antique restoration reality television shows. She could see that. Eric took the time to explain in great detail everything he was doing and to what purpose.

It was slow moving with having to rely on close-quarters fighting for the most part. You couldn't shoot a gun out here in the open, where it would carry for miles and draw in hundreds of the undead. Darlene was glad that John had finally stopped insisting that she use a bow and arrow, especially since the last time four days ago when she shot so wide that she'd almost hit an onlooker. She gripped her trusted machete and scanned the buildings and lots for enemies.

A zombie lumbered from Martin's restaurant, crashing through the mangled front door. Someone put an arrow between its eyes. Darlene didn't give it a second glance. She had ceased to even wonder whether or not they were male or female, young or old.

In the movies the zombies wore ironic uniforms like bloody nurses, hacked up lawyers and mutilated military men still wearing their helmets. Out here it was too hard to discern what profession they had been when alive. Their clothing was dirty, ripped and drab, covered in gore and dark stains.

Eric ran past her with a large meat cleaver in hand to cut off the zombie's head. Darlene just kept moving, trying her best to smell the salty air instead of the rot and decay. Her heels crunched through a bloodstained path and she looked away and made pretend it was the crunch of seashells underfoot.

A flock of seabirds cruised by on an updraft and they all stopped and watched as the creatures flew out of sight.

"I'd love to know where they're hiding," John said and everyone laughed.

The mood shifted as soon as they got around the bend and the RV's came into view. The wall stood twelve feet high in places, wood haphazardly nailed to the sides of the RVs to hook them together, cement and debris poured into the cracks between them.

Cars had been wedged in the gaps as well, with glass and rotting upholstery strewn across the street. Darlene looked away when she realized that body parts were also present.

"What's that noise?" someone asked as they got closer.

"They're on the other side." Eric ran ahead, scaling the steps of an RV and getting onto the roof in a single move. "Fuck," he managed.

Darlene and John got onto the top of another RV, helping others up. Whoever had put this together had done it smartly: the roofs had been reinforced with plywood and strips of steel and beams for support. Several rusting lawn chairs were bolted to the tops, a wind-ravaged plastic cooler on each roof.

The undead stood, thirty deep in places, trying to push forward. They could see more heading from the dunes on both sides and straight down A1A.

"Time to clear a path," John said and let loose with a volley of arrows.

Darlene could only stand off to the side and marvel at the proficiency of the bowmen in their group. She imagined that this is what the Middle Ages must have been like, with archers facing down the hordes of Mongols and Saxons. Something like that. She was never too clear on her ancient history, and supposed it didn't really matter now.

"This isn't working," John finally admitted. While there were two score undead lying motionless, another five score had wandered up and were waiting their turn. Bri was already digging into the second quiver of arrows and there were a handful of undead still up, arrow shafts jutting from shoulders, necks and chests.

"I'm going down," Darlene said and drew her machete again.

"I don't think so." John stared at Darlene.

"Please, daddy, please?" she said sarcastically before slipping down onto the small hood of the RV and dropping between three zombies. She quickly dispatched them and kicked away, giving her some room to move.

"Good idea," Eric said and drew his meat cleaver.

John, shaking his head, went back to firing arrows, working as close to Darlene as he could without accidentally hitting her again.

Eric and Darlene went back to back, the bodies piling up at their feet. Soon a gap was cleared, allowing the bowmen to shoot down the road as the zombies approached.

"Let's move onto the other side," John said. The group climbed down. "Darlene," John called.

"Yeah?"

"Don't do that again."

"Do what?" Darlene asked. She didn't bother to stop and talk to him, working her way forward as she spied another foe.

John ran and caught up with her. He put a hand on her shoulder. "That was stupid to jump down and you know it."

"You even said yourself that it wasn't working. I thought I'd either take the fight to them or wait until they rotted and hit the ground."

"Don't do that again," he repeated.

"Are you going to send me to my room now?"

Eric stepped in between them. "Can you two wait until we get back to do this? We have some company ahead."

"Fine," John and Darlene both said.

"You two need to get a room," Eric said with a laugh.

Chapter Eighteen

The road ahead was desolate, the pounding waves to their left and hulking, silent condominiums to their right. The nearest condo, its windows destroyed and doors flung open, looked ready to crash into the dirty swimming pool. A mangled corpse on a lounge recliner still took in the sun.

Darlene wondered how much longer she could go on like this. Running from the dead, going meal to meal and wondering if it would be her last, meeting the living and watching them die around her and then try to kill her. Was it all worth it anymore? Her stomach growled in answer. Even though she'd been eating better since joining this group, her weight was still down and her strength not what it once was. She felt like she was running out of time.

A zombie stumbled out from the dunes and was quickly dispatched with minimal effort from Eric.

Will I ever get back home? Is home still Maine, or is home wherever I stop? Is Maine still there *at this point?* Darlene felt a headache coming on and decided to live in the moment, as if that were possible. Shutting out the bad thoughts and the hopeful thoughts was sometimes just as hard as living this nightmare day to day.

John edged up to Darlene as they paced. "I'm sorry."

"For what?" Darlene smiled at him.

She knew she'd confused him and he stopped walking. "Huh?" he finally managed.

Darlene looked away from him. "You have to know that I care about you."

"I care about you, too."

She looked at him and dropped her smile. "You know that I *care* about you."

It was his turn to smile. "And I care about you."

"Are you this stupid?"

He stepped closer to her. "Right now, with everything going on… let's just get through today."

"How do we know there's going to be a tomorrow, John?"

He shrugged. "I guess we don't. But we have to try." John looked away at the ocean. "If I give up hope that my family is out there, somewhere, alive, what do I have?"

"You have this moment, you have people around you, surrounding you, that care for you now."

"You want to return to Maine. What if you found out Maine had fallen completely and there was nothing left there for you?"

"I'd either drop or I'd keep going. You can't base every action and every move on a what-if. You still need to get by. What if you found out she was gone, do you think she'd be happy to know that you then gave up? I think she'd want you to be happy and survive."

"I don't want to stop searching for her."

"Who said to?"

"It's just…"

"Getting involved with me, with anyone, doesn't mean you love her less or forgot about her. It just means you're living in the moment." Darlene leaned forward and kissed his cheek.

"I really care about you." John grabbed and hugged her, burying his face in her shoulder.

Darlene held him tightly as he sobbed. When Eric turned to investigate she waved him off and he nodded, moving away with the group.

John gently pushed away and wiped a tear from his eye. "Not very manly, I know."

"If you were a real cop I would have thought less of you. I've seen plenty of mall cops cry."

John laughed. "That's what I love about you."

They both stared awkwardly at one another before finally kissing.

Darlene closed her eyes and probed his mouth with her tongue, feeling his body respond and press against her. His hands gripped the small of her back. She wanted to enjoy this moment forever.

"Incoming," someone yelled.

John pushed her away and smiled. "You're a pretty good kisser for a makeup girl."

"I bet you say that to all the mall workers."

They jogged ahead and joined the group.

Eric had his binoculars out, studying the approaching group. "Damn, there must be hundreds of them." He smiled and handed the binoculars to John. "We might have found a couple thousand survivors."

A few people clapped and Bri hugged John.

"Okay, let's go meet our new friends. I'm sure they're tired, hungry and being followed by a horde of undead. We need to keep them moving, make sure no one has fallen behind, and half of us take up a rear position to keep the slower ones from getting lost."

"I'll take the rear guard," Darlene said. She'd walked many miles in this spot before. She felt elated just now, like she was accomplishing something positive in this negative world. "As cliché as that sounds," she whispered.

John got an arrow ready. "Watch for the undead coming from either side. With this many living moving and making noise, there's bound to be quite a few others coming to investigate."

"We just need to get them back into Flagler and we'll be safer there. A group from St. Augustine is coming up behind us and we'll hand the refugees off to them." Eric smiled. 'This is going to be a great day for mankind."

The small group came into sight of the mass within fifteen minutes, people stretching across the two lanes and over the dunes.

Bri began to wave and run ahead. Everyone smiled and laughed, the warm sun shining down on this wonderful scene.

Bri stopped in her tracks and turned back, only feet from the refugees. She looked at Darlene with panic in her eyes. "They're dead."

Indeed, hundreds and hundreds of recently deceased were shambling towards them.

Sons of The New Patriots

Doug Conrad tried his best to smile despite the six rifles pointing at his head and genitalia. "We seek sanctuary. We are starving. We have women with us who need help."

He noticed at least two rifles suddenly dip and point away from him. Doug loved horny dudes thinking with their genitalia. All it took was the mention of some pussy and they forgot about ass-fucking zombies and malnutrition and disease. You couldn't trump the lure of pussy.

He rubbed his face to look weary, but it was actually to keep them from seeing his smile. He knew that the gate to the shipyard would be opening any moment. They'd be cautious and take his weapons – but not his blade, they'd never find the blade – and escort him to their leader. They'd trade news of the outside world, trade a few weapons, foodstuffs, supplies, then the shipyard boys will get all friendly and see what it would involve to get a pussy or two for the evening. If it turned ugly or these shipyard boys were desperate and/or starving they'd simply try to kill them and take the supplies, food and women.

Doug knew that wasn't going to happen. Even now he had ten of his trusted men scaling fences and hiding on buildings, flanking the boys with the guns pointing at his balls. At a simple hand gesture they'd fire and kill anyone in the compound. Doug didn't want that. He didn't want the shooting. Not because he hated violence or bloodshed. He was simply tired of those fucking zombies that had been following them all the way from Orlando.

Central Florida had been a bust. As soon as they got there the damn internal strife of such a large, unorganized city had reared its head. Factions opposed to taking in new refugees clashed with the old-school save-everyone group.

The road from Connecticut had been long and deadly. Doug remembered all of his loyal men he'd lost over the months, especially in the beginning. He didn't believe in God but he believed that the human race had pissed someone or something off pretty fucking bad, and payback was such a bitch these days.

He'd learned early enough that despite the world being fucked, 'normal' people didn't trust bikers or militia. He'd ordered his loyalists to hide or remove their Sons of The New Patriots insignias and shirts to try to blend in with the locals and gain access. It was a waste of bullets and manpower to storm into a town and kill everyone just to find three bottles of swamp water and a half-eaten candy bar. Diplomacy had gotten them farther south than the noise of gunfire. Doug figured that close to a million undead were moving in his general direction from the northeast, and he wanted to keep moving away from them.

Without tipping his hand he glanced and saw that Rusty Byers was in position with his AK-47 to the left, in perfect range to kill everyone in the yard if it came down to that. He hoped it didn't, because any stray bullet could puncture a gas tank or punch a hole through one of the boats. They needed every boat they could get and as quickly as possible. He glanced back at the dozens of people milling about up the road, waiting for him to save them. Like a fucking messiah. Doug would sacrifice every last one of these losers to save himself and his loyalists. They were meat to him, trading pieces to get his way. Even the women were expendable, although he'd made a mental note of about ten that would be fun to fuck once they got onto the open water and had a brief respite.

Already, hundreds of the refugees had turned to the north and to 'freedom' in St. Augustine. He knew they'd never make it and he was surprised that they'd all managed to get this far. The old and the weak had been overrun as soon as they hit I-4 in Orlando, and that was the distraction that they needed to get away for the time being. But the undead didn't rest and they were still coming and picking up stragglers every mile with all of the damn noise thousands of people make.

A boat or two would get them north without having to fight a horde of zombies, and if there were women to fuck and food to eat, so much the better.

He wanted to yell out for them to hurry the fuck up, but decided not to. Instead he walked slowly in a circle and kicked at some pebbles on the road. He began counting backwards from one hundred. By the time he hit one, if they didn't open the gate, he would crack his knuckles and that would spark the bloodbath.

The people behind him thought he was a sound and honorable person. They thought he had been a simple school teacher in New Britain, Connecticut. They thought he had a loving wife and small child he was trying to find. They were sheep, stupid and easily lead by a stupid heart-wrenching story.

Before this was all over he would end up killing most of them, sparing only the ones who joined his cause. He'd rape as many of the women as he could before slitting their throats and leaving them for the zombies. That was just the way it had to be.

Fifty five... fifty four... fifty three...

Nothing personal. Doug Conrad needed to survive above all else. If he'd ever bothered to have a wife and kids he would have sacrificed them by now. No big deal. Prison had taught him about survival but the Sons of The New Patriots had taught him about getting what he wanted despite the corrupt government, God and the religious crazies interfering with his Constitutional rights, conservatives screaming about guns killing people, and the flood of minorities ruining the America he loved.

Ten... nine... eight...

"You can come in, but only you. Show us your hands and no funny business," one of the armed men yelled from the shipyard.

Funny business? There was going to be nothing funny about the way this played out. Doug put on a grim face and walked slowly into the compound.

They patted him down, missing his blade like the bunch of idiots that they were. "My name is Doug. We seek help."

"Shut up," one of the men said. He was dirty but looked well-fed, which was a great sign. There was food here. "Charlie will be out soon. Until then you need to shut up."

Doug nodded and wanted so bad to crack his knuckles but decided not to. No use in wasting a good bullet on this peon. He wanted to see who the fuck Charlie was and then go from there.

Charlie appeared within a few minutes and Doug was not impressed. He was old and walked with a cane, his gray hair and wispy beard framing his tired eyes and thin lips. He coughed into a liver-spotted hand as he stopped six feet from Doug and simply stared at him.

"I come seeking help," Doug finally said.

"You're not wanted here," Charlie croaked. "You need to take all of these dirty people with you."

One of Charlie's men whispered into his ear, pointing at the gates.

"I've no use for that," Charlie said.

"But the men do."

Doug couldn't help but smile. It always came down to the pussy. He decided to cut to the chase. "I have women with us, women who you can keep in exchange for two boats and supplies."

"How many?" Charlie asked.

Doug pointed back to the gate. "There are scores of them to choose from. Would ten suffice?"

The man next to Charlie spat on the ground. "There are twice as many men here."

Charlie shook his head. "You idiot," he muttered.

Doug grinned. "Twenty women for twenty men seems fair," he said loudly. "If we can just complete this deal and be on our way —"

"I'll have to think on it," Charlie said.

"We have no time for that. There's a horde of zombies following within minutes of us, and we'd just as soon leave."

Charlie glanced behind him at the gate. "We've counted at least a thousand people out there. How do you plan on getting a thousand people onto two boats?"

"I don't. I plan on getting as many as I can."

Charlie shook his head. "I don't believe you. If your intention was to save as many as you could, you would have asked for as many boats as we'd be willing to part with. Instead, you've already decided how many of these people will survive."

"That might be the case, but right now I'd just as soon make the deal and be on my way."

Charlie stared at Doug and scratched his cane into the dirt. "I'll think on it."

A scream from outside the compound shattered the moment.

Doug ran to the gate and could see the people pinned between the gates and the road behind them. Most began moving north, abandoning him and his plan.

"I need an answer now."

"When I am ready."

"Damn you, you've sentenced these people to die," Doug said.

"My loyalty lies with the people under my command and not some vagabonds that beg on my doorstep."

"Fuck you," Doug finally said. He cracked his knuckles and pulled the blade from the sleeve of his shirt.

The sound of quick gunfire sounded and bullets hit targets all around the yard. Before Doug could reach Charlie his head exploded.

"Get the gates," Doug yelled. "Follow the plan."

The gates were opened but as soon as people tried to enter they were met with guns in their face.

Doug strode forward. "Not so fast. We can only take a handful of you with us." He pointed at two women at the gate. "You two can come in."

As the two women ran past Doug a man called out to one of them and tried to enter. He was shot in the face.

"I decide who enters." Doug ignored the animalistic noises coming from the back of the refugees. Flanked by three gunmen, he began methodically picking women to enter.

"We need some men as well," Rusty said as he came up.

"Sorry, sometimes my dick gets the best of me." Doug pointed at three random men who looked like they could fight.

"What about the rest of us? Will you leave us to die?" someone screamed.

"I don't care what you do. Once we leave you're welcome to take the yard. But we need the supplies and the boats first."

A boy of no more than fourteen stepped forward carrying a skateboard. "I'm going."

Doug laughed. "I don't think so."

"Fuck you, old man; I'm going with you and the rest of your loser friends." The boy stared defiantly at Doug.

"You got balls, kid. Fuck it, you can come. Grab some supplies and let's get moving."

Finished with picking the survivors, they marched backwards towards the boats, making sure that no one tried to get past them or attack.

"We're ready to go. All aboard," Rusty called out.

They had to shoot a few people that tried to board the boats, but most people were simply plunging into the water or trying vainly to hide behind the remaining dry-docked boats and the few buildings.

As they pulled away from the dock, Doug stood on the deck and watched the chaos unfold, a smile etched on his weathered face.

Armand Rosamilia is a New Jersey boy currently living in sunny Florida, exactly in the area these stories take place... creepy. He writes all day (and sometimes at night), and has amassed over 70 releases to date, with many many more on the horizon.

Want to buy all of his books so he can get fatter, sitting around in Flagler Beach, eating cinnamon raisin bagels with tuna and drinking banana bread beer?

http://armandrosamilia.com will get you all the details. He likes tips and bags of M&M's as well...

DYING DAYS 2

ARMAND ROSAMILIA

HIGHWAY TO HELL

ARMAND ROSAMILIA

DYING SHORTLY 2

DYING DAYS: ORIGINS 2

HIGHWAY TO HELL 2

DYING DAYS: ORIGINS

HIGHWAY TO HELL